W9-CHF-779

Duo
and
Le Toutounier

Also By Colette

THE EVENING STAR

JOURNEY FOR MYSELF: SELFISH MEMORIES

THE OTHER WOMAN *(Stories)*

PLACES

THE THOUSAND AND ONE MORNINGS

RETREAT FROM LOVE

LOOKING BACKWARDS

TRANSLATED FROM THE FRENCH AND

WITH AN INTRODUCTION BY

Margaret Crosland

The Bobbs-Merrill Company, Inc.

Indianapolis/New York

Published by the Bobbs-Merrill Company, Inc.
Indianapolis New York
Published in Great Britain by Peter Owen Limited
ISBN 0-672-51849-X
Library of Congress catalog card number 74-21145
Designed by Jacques Chazaud
Manufactured in the United States of America

First printing

Introduction

In 1934, when *Duo* was first published in France, Colette had already written fourteen novels and many other books, mainly autobiographical in essence. *Duo* was adapted for the stage in 1938 by Paul Geraldy, and Colette herself was touched—jealous, too, she said—when the play was a success. The story also made a discreet appearance in English with minor expurgations and a hero called Michael.

Colette obviously saw her novel as a husband-and-wife duet or dialogue and, while none of her books are crowded with characters, Alice and Michael have the stage to themselves here. Only the servant, Maria, is given a speaking part; the ex-lover is confined to old letters and exchanges—although the reader hears nothing—over the long-distance telephone. Colette had decided to examine a marriage, and nothing, nobody, could be allowed to obscure the marital situation. She was even prepared to use unlikely coincidence, as well as a touch of melodrama, to protect her characters from the outside world. Occasionally the reader, like Alice herself, is allowed some fresh air in the grounds of the house in which the novel is set.

The existence of children rarely inconveniences Colette's characters, but in this story and its sequel, *The Toutounier*, the heroine Alice and her sisters, experienced as they are in many things, hardly seem grown up. They speak an amusing private language, invented, according to her third husband, Maurice Goudeket, by Colette herself. He remembers that a variant of the intriguing, intimate-sounding, untranslatable title-word was used by the artist Luc-Albert Moreau as an affectionate name for his wife, Helene Jourdan-Morhange, the violinist. The short novel was published in 1939 and, like many books appearing in that year, did not receive the attention it deserved, although the perceptive critic Edmond Jaloux declared it one of his favorites among Colette's work. The English critics John Weightman and Martin Turnell have subsequently rated both *Duo* and *The Toutounier* as being among Colette's best work.

Jaloux invoked Maupassant and the illuminating value of the "humble truth," saying that the fascination of *The Toutounier* was to be found in "minute, poignant, profoundly sad things which lie beyond everyday observation and touch upon the most deeply concealed areas of our lives." A whole generation later we notice not so much the things that are "profoundly sad"—perhaps we are conditioned to this aspect of Colette's work—as her obsessive preoccupation with women characters. She had always preferred to describe and cherish women, whereas the only men characters who interested her were the very young—Cheri, then the heroes of *Ripening Seed* and *The Cat*. She did not attack the "beloved enemy," as she had once described men. They hardly deserved so much attention, and she, or at least her heroines, apparently regarded them as ineffectual, selfish and vain. When she wrote *Duo* and its sequel she used three heroines and a servant to express in random acidulated sentences all she felt on the subject: did any man ever do what you expected him to do; the hardest thing in life was making sure of a man; a husband must have his revenge, simply because he is a husband. In fact, men have a bad press.

As for the women characters, they are hard-working and self-reliant, but self-indulgent also, obsessed with their bodies, clothes and material surroundings. They need men, but show little sign of loving them and tend to prefer work, if only out of habit and even if they grumble about it. Alice and her sisters cannot escape from their adolescence for long and, if the mother-figure who pervades so much of Colette's non-fiction is absent here, the indestructible *toutounier* is both womb and gynaecium, the women's quarters, the only comfortable, comforting place.

The two books were written at a time when women in France had few rights and usually worked—if they could not avoid work—in only a few professions of limited "feminine" interest. Marriage or a respectable liaison were considered more worthwhile. Most of Colette's women reserved for themselves the right to do what they wanted to do. They would never have carried banners for any so-called liberation movement, but they tend to slip away from the male chauvinists or give them only half of themselves, insisting on their own chaotic or lonely individualism backed by their solidarity *tra donne sole*. In earlier novels Colette's characters had contemplated giving all for love or had even done so, but, realists like their creator, they found that love was difficult, marriage more or less unworkable.

In these two stories, Colette spoke more clearly, in her quiet, ironic way, than in many of her better known novels. *Duo* and *The Toutounier* bring out all the sharpness in that rich, inimitable voice.

M.C.

Duo

He thrust the door open and stood for a moment on the threshold. "Oh my goodness!" he sighed. Groping his way across the room, he collapsed onto the divan and immersed himself completely in the cool shade. But he preferred recriminations to rest, so he heaved himself upright.

"He didn't spare me a single thing! Chevestre dragged me everywhere. Just look at my shoes. The cowshed's falling down on top of the cows, the osier beds are flooded, and the neighbor across the river's fishing with cartridges. Just listen, I had to . . ."

He interrupted himself.

"You look very pretty here. That deserves consideration, obviously."

His wife had placed the unattractive old bureau across the deep window recess, catching the midday sunshine that was starry with floating dust. A bunch of purple orchis stood in a thick little troughlike vase in front of her, showing that Alice had just come back from the dampest part of the meadows, which were softly carpeted with alder and osier roots. Beneath her hand lay a leather blotter of the same color as the flowers, and the light from it was reflected onto Alice's face, disturbing the gray-green color of her eyes, which Michel used to compare to willow leaves.

She listened to her husband understandingly and answered him only with a sleepy smile. He never tired of relishing the fact that Alice's eyes and mouth, when extended by her smile, acquired almost the same length and shape.

"When you're here there's a lot of red-gold in your hair," said Michel. "In Paris it's black."

"And white," said Alice. "Ten, twenty white hairs there, on top . . ."

She turned her forehead toward the light and lied coquettishly. She was proud of being a young and nonchalant thirty-seven, proud of her slim figure. She saw that Michel was getting up to come over to her.

"No, Michel! Your shoes! Think of the floor; they polished it this morning! All that red mud!"

The sound of her voice always won Michel over. It was sleepy too, and slightly querulous, capable of protesting gently, in the same key, against good and bad. Michel moved his legs apart to form a V and carefully allowed only his heels to touch the broad, well-worn floorboards.

"This red mud, my dear, comes from the river banks. I'm a hero; I left here in a hurry at nine o'clock and I've only sat down once since then, to drink some white wine, and what wine! A greenish, poisonous white it was, just right for cleaning brass or sharpening knives."

He stood up with a slight effort and placed a hand across the small of his back.

"My dear, it's the price we pay for our holidays. Shall we still be the bosses here in 1934? That man Chevestre . . . he's got an acquisitive look on his face, Chevestre—while as for me. . . . How much longer will I look like a property owner?"

He walked up and down, his steps leaving dry muddy marks behind him, but Alice was no longer thinking about the floor.

"You look all right as you are!" She tossed the words at him as he passed in front of the bureau.

She hadn't accustomed him to such sharp rejoinders; he stopped and smiled at her.

"Are things as bad as that, Michel?" From the entreaty in Alice's voice he realized her need for reassurance, and he reassured her.

"No, my dear, not as bad as that. No worse than anywhere else. But what can one do? The roofing's had its day; the way they work at the farm is fifty years out of date. I don't think Chevestre cheats more than any other manager . . . we'll have to choose; we'll have to set all our money aside, everything that the Petit-Casino Theatre brings in, for restoring and reinforcing Cransac. When I think that only three years ago a film would run for five months, and that every winter we put on a revue in the provinces with what was left of Jeanne Rasimi's costumes . . . when I think . . ."

Alice stopped him again by stretching out her hand, fingers together.

"No, don't think about it. That's precisely what we mustn't think about. The osiers . . ."

"They've split. They won't even bring in three thousand francs."

"But why did they split?"

He looked down at her, as he enjoyed doing when she was sitting and he was standing, with fitting sympathy.

"Why? My poor dear, don't you know?"

"No. Do you?"

He laughed, suddenly and quietly.

"No, I don't know either. I don't understand anything about them. Chevestre says it's the heat. But Maure, the tenant, says definitely that if Chevestre had had them cut hard back two years ago. . . . And he also says the ground's too solid for osiers. You can imagine how much I know about it."

He raised his hand, holding his little finger up in the air as though he were playing a game of forfeits. Then he stopped laughing and talking and stood facing the French windows. A springtime upsurge of new leaves, unpruned shoots and long rose suckers, flushed by the apoplectic sap, brought the neglected groups of shrubs closer to the house. On the poplars the gold and bronze of the new leaves still wrongfully occupied the place of the green. A crabapple tree, its white petals lined with bright red, had defeated the somewhat sickly Judas tree, and the syringas, in their attempt to escape the destructive shade of the shiny aucubas, extended their slender branches and their butter-white stars through the broad, grasping leaves, which were mottled like snakes.

Michel gauged the width of the walk, which had been narrowed by the advancing beds of shrubs—no one pruned them any longer—and the mixture of species.

"They're fighting each other," he said softly. "If you look at them too often it's not funny anymore . . ."

"What isn't?"

Half-turning around in her chair, she compared Michel to the Michel of the past. *No better, and no worse . . .* When they were standing they were the same height, but she looked very tall and he somewhat short. He made more play than she did with a totally physical seductiveness, a youthfulness of gesture, both qualities due to the fact that he had been in two or three professions where he'd been forced to please both men and women.

When he spoke he revealed his well-cared-for teeth, his tobacco-colored eyes. He had recently grown a little chin-strap beard to conceal the relaxed throat beneath his chin; it was soft and curly, very short, and looked as though it were painted on his skin up to his ears, and as a result, with his low forehead and rounded curls, his not very prominent nose and full lips, he resembled one of those fine antique heads.

Alice was drawing and secretly watching him. She was particularly afraid that he was going to tell her about too many disturbing topics all at once. The fine weather and a gentle tingling bodily fatigue made her feel cowardly; she wanted only to remain unaware that with each storm the roof lost a few lichen-gilded tiles and that in the cowshed they stuffed up the holes in the walls with straw rather than send for the builder. In Paris at least she didn't think about it.

"And what else?" she asked in spite of herself.

Michel sat up and muttered like a man being wakened from sleep or trying to gain time.

"What? What else? . . . Nothing else. Chevestre only talks about tiresome things—you know that. Three hours of problems when we arrive, three hours of problems the day before we leave; one or two little setbacks while we're here—that's the price I pay for our Easter holidays. Is it expensive or not?"

He passed behind his wife, leaned against the rotting window frame and breathed in the smell of the place where he had been born. The soft, violet-colored earth, the grass that had already grown long, the catalpa in flower above the red hawthorn, the sweetbrier raining down over the entrance to the French windows, the syringas which had been brought forward by the heat, laburnum flowers hanging down in long yellow strands. He did not want to lose a single one of these fresh, neglected and ancient possessions. But the only thing to which he clung to an unreasonable extent was Alice. In the distance the invisible, swollen river, which was still cold, streamed in the sunshine like smoke from burning weeds.

"Chevestre would pay a high price. He wants the place, the bastard. His campaign's been well organized. My neighbor Capdenac warned me: When your manager starts to wear boots, put him out, or else he'll get *you* out. . . ."

A slender hand was placed on his sleeve: "It's not expensive; it costs nothing," said Alice.

Without getting up, she had turned her chair halfway around toward the window, toward the place where sunshine, the sound of buzzing, the clucking of hens and the song of nightingales came in. The low ceiling with its brown beams, the dark colors of the furniture and the sprigged covers with their brown background, swallowed up the light and gave out only faint reflected gleams on the belly of a big Oriental vase, a copper jug or the beveling of an Italian mirror. Alice lived in this library dining room, but she restricted herself to the space between the French windows and the fireplace, avoiding the dark areas at the back of the room and the two vast bookcases without glass which went up to the ceiling.

"You're nice," said Michel briefly, stroking his wife's smooth head. He felt vulnerable, on the point of becoming sentimental, and wanted to hide the fact. "I'm worn out! I was tired anyway, and it's the climate here! This place is hotter than Nice, I'll bet."

Because he'd directed theatre "seasons" in casino towns, he'd kept the habit of comparing everything to Nice, Monte Carlo or Cannes. But he didn't dare do it aloud anymore, at least not in front of Alice, who would knit her brows and wrinkle up her catlike nose, scolding him in plaintive tones: "Michel, don't talk like an estate-agent!"

The rounded head accepted the caress of his skillful

hand. This was because Michel knew how to stroke it the right way, following Alice's hair style, which never changed: she always had a thick fringe, parallel to her horizontal eyebrows, and no curls. She wore daring dresses, but a strange timidity prevented her from altering the arrangement of her hair.

"That's enough, Michel; you're tiring me . . ."

He bent down over the attractive upturned face which was only lightly made up and refused to age; over the eyes which closed so quickly, both in boredom and in excessive happiness.

If Cransac were sold, I'd recover. Even without repairs, Cransac's a terrible burden. If it were sold I'd feel free. I'd pay more attention to Alice's comfort. I'd still beaver away for her . . . for the two of us. . . . When he talked to himself he readily used old slang words, just as he would move his shoulders up and down unnecessarily, indicating his struggle for existence.

"You're very touchy this morning. You weren't like that last night . . ."

She didn't protest, but all she revealed of her glance now was a thin line of bluish white between her blackened eyelashes and her smiling mouth. He caressed her with a few crude words, which she heard with a quiver of her eyelashes, as though he had shaken a wet bunch of flowers over her. They both accepted these exchanges, which were caused by chance, travel, a sudden change of season. They had arrived the previous day during a springtime storm; at Cransac they had found rain, the sunset, a rainbow over the river, heavy-hanging lilacs, the moon rising in a green sky, shiny little frogs under the stone steps, and during the night more showers, but less violent, and large drops of nightingale song falling from the top of the wood. . . .

Just as her husband was clasping her head and warm shoulder against him, and crushing her chin in a hand that had lost its gentleness, Alice pushed him away, warning him in a low voice:

"Maria's coming! It's half past twelve!"

"So what? Let her come. She's caught us more than once!"

"Yes, but I've never liked it. Neither has she. Straighten your pullover. Tidy your hair a bit . . ."

"Don't worry," said Michel. "Let's look natural. *Acré,* the cops are coming!"

Alice never laughed when her husband made certain heavy jokes; she knew what words he was going to use. But she showed no impatience about it, having accepted all his vulgarity, which he emphasized on purpose, and his concealed fastidiousness. "I don't like it when you're subtle," she would tell him. "You're only subtle when you're unhappy."

In the distance the warped floorboards creaked under Maria's footsteps. She pushed the door open roughly and revealed only half of herself.

"Does Madame want me to ring the first bell for luncheon?"

"What about me? Don't I count, you old insect?" joked her master.

She looked more like a horse, but the way grasshoppers do with their horselike foreheads. She laughed, thanked Michel with a wink from her glittering little eye, and closed the rebellious door.

Alice, who had stood up, was putting her pencils away.

"You certainly work hard at winning over Maria."

"Are you jealous?" said Michel quickly, in his best *table d'hôte* manner.

His wife didn't condescend to reply. With the flat of her hand she made certain that her smooth hair, with its off-center style, was in place. She knew that Maria, the housekeeper, accepted no other authority, no other flattery, but Michel's. Maria, who was lean and sharp, put on a splendid act, at the age of fifty, as Michel's old nurse. She was very good at clasping her hands and sighing: "If you didn't know him when he was young, you've seen nothing!" In fact, she'd only worked for him for ten years, and the reason she sometimes regarded Alice as an equal was that they had come to Cransac during the same year. But Alice was fair to Maria, who looked after Cransac with honest vigilance, assisted only by her husband, a robust but weak-willed handyman who was discouraged by the thirty acres of garden.

"Shall we wash our hands?" asked Michel.

"Yes, but in the kitchen. Everything's clean in the bathroom. I forbid you to go in. I've even done the taps."

He laughed, teasing her for being eccentric.

"What about Maria? Do you think she'll like our washing at 'her' sink?"

Lazily she turned toward him her dark head and her fine gray eyes that looked green in the dazzling light from the window.

"No. But Maria knows that she sometimes has to hide what she doesn't like. Where are you going with those flowers?"

He was skillfully carrying the thick little glass vase brimming over with wild orchis.

"To the table, actually. The purple light looked so pretty in your eyes and on your cheeks . . . like that. But we need that other thing too; it's the same color—you know what I mean?"

"What other thing? Look out, Michel—you're spilling the water from the flowers . . . are you coming?"

"I've never knocked over a vase of flowers in all my life! Some kind of blotter—it was there, on your bureau . . . it isn't there anymore. Have you put it away? What were you doing with it? Were you writing?"

"No, I was just making a few odd sketches for costumes."

"Costumes for what?"

She looked at him as though from a distance, excusing herself with a half-smile: "Oh, you know . . . I just enjoy it. I always tell myself that if *Daffodyl* goes on next season, my costumes wouldn't be more expensive; in fact, they'd probably cost less than using the old Mogador costumes again, and without boasting . . ."

She extended her long hand, with its fingers together, and completed her sentence with a nod of her head.

"Show me!" ordered Michel impetuously, and he

placed the little vase on the bureau. "Where are your sketches? In the purple blotter?"

Alice snapped her fingers impatiently.

"Come on, please! What is all this? There's no purple blotter! Let's have lunch, Michel!"

He looked at his wife with an injured expression.

"Just listen! There's no purple blotter! Speaking to me like that, as though I were a child!"

He raised his arm and indicated the spot on Alice's cheek from where the reflection had disappeared.

"There . . . and there . . ." he said, half to himself. "The color was well worth painting. You seemed to be lit by red footlights, with one-third of the bulbs blue . . . red . . . violet . . . wonderful . . ."

She shrugged her shoulders, her expression uncomprehending. "I'm going to have lunch, Michel. The quiche will be cold."

"Wait!"

The sound of his voice, much more than the command, held her back. Michel had uttered a strange cry on a tenor note. She knew the reasons for such a change of timbre. As she turned around she saw that Michel looked slightly green and was breathing rapidly. She allowed herself the time and the indulgence to think: *He looks like Mathô, but a smaller version . . .* Then she entered calmly into the unknown.

"Whom are you complaining about, Michel?"

He shook his curly head, as though to reject everything she was going to say.

"Don't make complications. There's something

odd . . . quick, Alice . . . you say there's no blotter, no . . . purple thing here. I'm not going out of my mind. Repeat what you said. . . . Isn't there one?"

She looked desperately at her husband's disordered face and the dark rings that had suddenly appeared around his eyes. She glanced quickly at the walls, between the beams in the ceiling, for some stray gleam of light, some purple flash reflected from a mirror, a prismatic exchange between two edges of cut glass. Finding nothing, she looked back at Michel.

"No," she said sadly.

She observed him with so much anxiety that he was taken in. He exhaled deeply and flopped into Alice's armchair.

"My goodness, how tired I am . . . whatever happened? What's the matter with me?"

He looked up at her like a child, and she almost let herself go, almost took him in her arms, wept a little and trembled within his protection. She only allowed herself to do what caution demanded of her. She composed a gentle, astonished smile for herself, made an effort to open her long eyes and keep them fixed on Michel's beseeching gaze.

"But you frightened me, Michel," she said plaintively.

He looked at her with the anxious, uncompromising love that many frivolous men devote in secret to a faithful companion, and he sighed with relief at seeing her so like herself, her mouth barely touched with lipstick, her lower lip broad and often chapped, her upper lip short and drawn up by her nose—that little nose that was slightly flat, slightly crushed, ugly, Cambodian and inimitable—and those eyes especially, elongated like leaves, with their mingled green and gray, pale in the evening by lamplight, darker in the morning.

She didn't move or look away. But Michel saw that under the thick fringe of her hair one of Alice's eyebrows was dancing imperceptibly up and down in the grip of a little nervous tremor. At the same time his nostrils detected the scent that revealed emotion, the sweat dragged cruelly out of the pores by fear, by anguish, the scent which caricatured the perfume of sandalwood, of heated boxwood, the perfume reserved for the hours of love and the long days of high summer. He unclasped the two consoling arms, half-turned around and opened the bureau drawer.

The leather blotter shone in the ray of sunlight that touched it, and Michel's first reaction was one of childish victory.

"Do you see? Well?"

Because he was smiling as he repeated, "Well? . . . well? . . ." Alice took care to smile too. She was hardly thinking of anything, concentrating only on remaining motionless. *If I don't move, he won't move either . . .* But as soon as she smiled his expression changed, and she saw clearly that Michel's smile was without significance. She used the only excuse available to her and said:

"The first bell's gone."

He turned mechanically toward the French windows, crooking his neck as though to see the little black bell that was half-buried by the red May tree and the yellow jasmine, and Alice hoped he was going to take himself in hand again and get up, conscious of the delay, knowing Maria and the delayed luncheon, that he would put off until later what he had to know, say and do. *Later,* she said to herself, *I'll have sorted everything out. Or else we'll be dead.*

She risked a half-turn toward the door, but Michel held her by the wrist.

"Wait!" he said. "It's not over yet."

She cheated, cried out aloud, and tried to burst into tears. "You're hurting me! Let me go!"

She turned her wrist in his hand, which opened immediately, and gave up hope of being roughly handled, for Michel kept his sang-froid in an abnormal way, like a drowning man who says as he swallows salt water: "What a pity! I'd only worn those cufflinks twice!" He showed her an attentive, alert face, for in reality he was no more than alert and attentive, still as full of hope as she was; he was fighting for her and not against her. For a moment he made himself behave, as she used to say, "nicely," with his head on one side, and a somewhat crestfallen half-smile in his tobacco-colored eyes.

She felt herself grow old in a few moments. *I won't be able to save him from what he's afraid of,* she thought, and in her disheartened state she began to hate him. She relaxed, sat back on one leg and realized that her reaction constituted a kind of surrender.

He still didn't open the purple blotter, however, and Alice had time to read within Michel a cowardly urge, exactly like her own, to close the drawer, to chase and catch a moment that was running away from them, leaving them rigid, forgotten and motionless, the moment when Michel had mentioned the purple reflection on Alice's cheek. *I'm going to call out to him: it's a game! I'm going to take the blotter and run away; he'll run after me, and . . .*

Michel, his head very close to Alice's throbbing breasts, asked timidly, "What's inside it?"

She shrugged her shoulders feebly and bent down toward him as though to bid him good-bye.

"Nothing. Nothing, now."

He clutched at the last two words in a fury! "So you've had time to get rid of everything, then?"

She sat up straight, took a deep breath, dilating her Cambodian nostrils, then ran her tongue over her broad chapped lip, and her face grew younger. So there had to be a discussion; she had to defend herself, make diplomatic admissions, hurt Michel in order to keep him occupied, so that he didn't hurt himself too much. *Make good what I've done. . . . What got hold of me; what made me say there was no purple blotter? My poor, poor Michel . . .*

She held back the tears which gave a vivid brilliance to her eyes, and the blood mounted to her cheeks. She modestly pressed her elbows against her sides because of the damp patch that was spreading under her arms and making a dark stain on her blue dress.

"Listen, Michel. You must understand . . ."

He laughed unkindly, raising his hand.

"Oh, my goodness . . . oh no . . . that would surprise me . . ."

She had often known him to be deceptively relaxed like this during some business deal and laugh in the same way when he had thought everything lost.

"Michel, if you don't open that blotter you'll be doing the right thing; there's nothing in it any longer, neither for you nor for me. If you open it, the—er—the piece of paper you'll find in it, tell yourself firmly that it's nothing, nothing anymore. A—just ashes, just what's left of something that's all over, finished. . . . Nothing, in fact, you understand. Nothing . . ."

He listened to her in astonishment, his eyebrows raised, and tugged with two fingers at his new little chin-strap beard with an incredulous expression. But he heard what was essential:

"Finished, you say? Oh, well . . . good . . ."

He seized the smooth leather blotter which reflected the sunlight like a mirror. A patch of purple leaped up to the ceiling and quivered between the brown beams. When Michel opened the blotter a thin sheet of paper glided down obliquely to the floor, between the feet of the bureau. Alice placed her hand on Michel's sleeve.

"Won't you just leave it there? I'll throw it away, I'll burn it, and . . . Michel, think of us . . ."

He bent down with some effort and, as he rose, looked at her furiously. He was angry with her for having forced him, by appearing too upset, to pick up that flimsy sheet of paper, which rustled in a metallic way in his hand like a new banknote as he felt it mechanically. "It's foreign paper, the paper people use when they write ten or fifteen pages to each other . . ."

However, the sheet carried only a few lines of very fine handwriting.

"But that's Ambrogio's writing!"

Alice sensed how much hope there was in his naïve cry, and felt that the harshest moment was coming. She reached the divan and sat down, not folding her long legs beneath her as she usually did, but sitting upright, ready to rise to her feet and run. The wisdom and foresight of her body frightened her; with a glance she measured the distance from the divan to the window, and lost patience. *Well, hasn't he read it yet? What's he waiting for? We can't spend the whole day like this. . . .*

"Ambrogio . . ." repeated Michel. "What's the date of this letter?"

"November 1932," she said briefly.

"November 1932? Wasn't I at Saint-Raphaël in November last year?"

She shrugged her shoulders, outraged that he was straining his eyes and looking for his round spectacles.

"On the letter rack," she said curtly, in the same dry voice.

"What?"

"Your spectacles are on the letter rack, I tell you!"

She was gradually becoming exasperated, gradually

recovering the desire to criticize and to fight back. *Good heavens, how stupid he looks! But he knows he can't read Ambrogio's writing without spectacles! Do I have to read it aloud to him?*

He moved awkwardly, as though he were naked, and took a long time to hook the curved arms of his spectacles behind his ears. She felt he was humiliated, on the point of becoming furious in order to save face, and she took good care to show no expression. Moreover, he changed as soon as he had glanced at the letter, which Alice read to herself from memory at the same time.

"I don't even dare thank you for such an evening, such a night, Alice. I hardly dare remember the gift you gave me, and still go on begging. It's too wonderful, too lovely . . . I clasp your whole body in my arms."

She waited for Michel to raise his eyes and look at her, and she thought, a little at a time, in a detached way: *How slow it all is; he's taking a long time. And that idiot who went and wrote my name in his first letter. Such a corny letter. The following ones were better, it's true. I should have told Michel just anything. It was the childhood of art. The arthood of child. Just when I was going to tear it up; it's bad luck. That'll teach me. I swear that if everything settles down without a catastrophe I'll go to bed and sleep until tomorrow morning. . . .*

When he'd finished reading, he folded his spectacles and looked at his wife. At first she felt great relief that he'd become handsome once again and emerged from any hesitation.

"Well?" said Michel in a brittle voice.

"Well?" she repeated, feeling injured.

"Well, I'm waiting for you to explain yourself."

She didn't admit the interrogatory tone at first. Out of diplomacy she gave free rein to her anger. Her little Asiatic nose grew broader; she knitted her brows, and her thick fringe came down to her eyelashes.

"Is any explanation necessary?" she said calmly.

Unconsciously he imitated his wife's change of expression. He lowered his eyebrows and returned Alice's angry half-smile, baring his short teeth.

"Just additional information. I see you've got the good taste not to deny it. I beg you, don't try to look like a little Annamite boy who's stolen something—that doesn't impress me anymore. So it amounts to this: Ambrogio, while I was killing myself for the Saint-Raphaël Casino, after entrusting him with the Avenue cinema . . . it's not very old, this business. It's quite new, it seems to me?"

"No," she said disparagingly. "I've told you it doesn't exist any longer. I could add that it barely existed at all."

He assumed a knowing expression. "That's what you say!"

She made no reply. She was thinking over the way their conversation had taken a turn for the worse. She had hoped for a rapid solution with tears, reproaches, two cruel hands around her wrists, a vase smashed. . . . She listened for Maria's footsteps and thought about the little black bell. . . . *When the second bell rings, what's going to happen? Oh, if I hadn't stopped Michel from kissing me when he came back, I know very well where we'd be now. What an idiot I am.*

She turned her head toward the door at the back of the room, flanked by the two vast bookcases, toward the bedroom where the twin beds stood beneath a single fringed canopy, and cursed herself more violently. *Laziness about taking off a dress, or pulling it up! Being careful so that Maria won't know we've crumpled the chintz on the bed, made the bathroom "dirty" again! And now. . . .*

She waited for Michel to turn around; he was standing in front of the French windows, which the sun was gradually leaving. In the end he did turn and show Alice a face she recognized, his pleasant, everyday face, tired, still attractive, so little capable of expressing sadness.

"My dear girl, what have you done to us with this?"

She was taken unawares and had to fight against her rising tears, the sob that made her cough, the salty saliva that tasted of blood, the female desire to ruin her appearance and beseech him. She could only stammer:

"Michel . . . I assure you . . . my dear Michel . . ."

At the same moment the black bell above the window shook the strands of laburnum and made its imperious, frenzied little voice heard. Alice rose quickly, pulled her dress tidy and smoothed her hair. Michel cursed under his breath and consulted his wristwatch.

"That's the second bell," said Alice.

"And it's late, too," said Michel. "Oh . . ."

He made a despairing gesture and Alice guessed that he was thinking of Maria, of Maria's husband, of Chevestre, of the neighboring village, all those familiar, skillful spies.

"What shall we do?" she asked in a low voice. But she consulted him especially with her eyes and surveyed him with the fine glance of a humble accomplice. He shrugged his shoulders and thrust his hands into his pockets. "We'll go to table, naturally . . ."

He stood aside for her to pass, stopped her, and looked at her closely:

"Put some powder on . . . you've got some black, there, under your eye. No, not with your finger—you'll make it worse. Be careful, for goodness' sake!"

He offered her his handkerchief.

She had imagined that luncheon would be a complicated form of torture, a travesty of a meal, both of them paralyzed with embarrassment and hypocritical ease. But she was astounded to see that Michel was occupied solely in hiding things from Maria. As he went into the dining room, which always had a slightly moldy, cellarlike smell, he cried, "Oh ho! What do I see? Radishes already? Are they hothouse radishes, then?"

Alice looked at him from where she sat as though he had made some unsuitable remark, but Maria condescended to laugh, and Michel went on seeking the same success by the same methods. He questioned the unbending servant about the vegetable garden and learned, with passionate interest, that a swarm of bees were building their combs under the old tiled roof; and when Maria described the death of a sheepdog that he had seen only twice, he heaved a theatrical sigh: "My poor old fellow!" In the meantime he poured out the sparkling cider for his wife, passed her the bread, and said, "Oh, sorry," as though he were making polite small talk.

He's really trying too hard, thought Alice, who was shocked. *All that for Maria! He'll make her suspicious! In any case, he already has. She senses everything.*

As though she were reading, Maria's eyes went from the talkative Michel to the silent Alice, who was eating hungrily, husbanding her strength. A crumpled, damp little handkerchief by Alice's plate attracted Maria's gaze as though it were a gold coin.

"Would Madame like coffee here? If Madame's tired, perhaps Madame would be more comfortable in the library?"

Maria addressed Alice in the third person, but she said "You" to Michel with exaggerated, peasantlike familiarity.

"That's it," said Michel approvingly. "Excellent idea. Coffee in the library."

"Would you like some *marc,* Monsieur?"

"What? Would I like some *marc?* What a question! Hey, Alice, she's asking if I'd like some *marc!* You go in: I'll hold the door. Maria, *sancta Maria, gratia plena,* won't you ever get around to having this door seen to?"

Alice went back into the library without saying a word. She was shaking with fury and reacted with violent language. *It's beneath contempt,* she thought. *This play-acting for the sake of a servant. He's terrified she'll know he's a deceived husband! And to think I was dreading . . . just anything. Well, I needn't worry. Oh, I hate . . . I hate everything.* She picked up the coffeepot clumsily and almost wept because the coffee spurted on to the sugar.

"My child, you're trembling all over! Come on, I'm not going to kill you . . ."

He followed the movement of her long unsteady hand, and Alice weakened beneath the kind, caressing voice, raising an appreciative face toward her husband. *How tired he is, too. It's killing me, this tiredness. I'm falling asleep where I stand, that's what's the matter with me. . . .*

Michel shook his head intelligently. "That kind of gratitude doesn't suit you. What did you think I was going to do? Smash the place up and throw you out? Tell the whole neighborhood?"

She half-closed her eyes again and once more assumed her nearsighted, remote expression.

"Oh no, not that . . ."

He sensed the dubious implications of her reply, let his chin jut forward and thrust his clenched fists into his pockets.

"It might have been a good thing if I'd . . . Don't think we won't talk about this business again . . ."

He exhaled deeply in a self-important, apoplectic

way and strode toward the window from where the sunshine was retreating. The birds were following the light, and the bees had deserted the deep recess. On the table-top bureau lay the purple blotter, its glow extinguished.

It's almost evening already . . . Alice shivered with fatigue, half-stretched out on the divan and threw over her legs the tartan rug that spent the whole year at Cransac, full of mothholes and burned by cigarettes smoked at siesta time.

If I ask him for a cigarette, will he take it as a show of bravado, or a sign of guilty unconcern? . . . She didn't take her eyes away from Michel's back and shoulders as he stood in front of the French windows. *He's acting like a bull. He's snorting and puffing. Maybe he's furious. Maybe he's cold, in fact. You never knew with these half-Southerners. Has everything been spoiled, and is it my fault? It's barely an hour since everything changed, but I can't stand it any longer. If I were sure he's not suffering I'd give up. I'd take a hot-water bottle and go to bed. But if he's suffering it's not possible, it's unfair, it's ridiculous. Michel, my darling Michel . . .*

He turned around just at the moment when she was mentally calling him, and for that small miracle she almost held her arms out to him.

"No," he said, returning to his threatening attitude. "You mustn't think it's all over. It's only just beginning."

She closed her pale eyes, let her head lie against a faded silk cushion, and raised her hand.

"Listen, Michel. This . . . stupid thing I did—"

"This shameful thing!" he said violently, without raising his voice.

"This shameful thing, fine; whatever you say. This shameful thing that occurred briefly in my life when you weren't there began and ended in less than four weeks. What? No, no! You shan't interrupt me all the time!" she cried suddenly, opening her eyes again. In the shadow they looked almost blue. "You'll let me have my say!"

He leaped silently over to the half-open door and closed it carefully, without making a sound.

"Are you crazy? They're having lunch there in the kitchen. One might think . . . one might really think . . . for heaven's sake! And what about the postman, who must be on his way up the hill?"

He was stammering, shouting under his breath, carefully suppressing his anger. Vehemently he extended his arm toward the French windows, and Alice noticed that he opened his mouth in a square shape, like the tragic masks of old. But she shook her shoulders violently and went on:

"And what about the little cowhand: have you forgotten him? And Chevestre—he must surely be listening somewhere? And the girl from the post office, she's probably put her on best hat to come and ask you to recommend her for promotion? Tell me, are you afraid of them? Do they matter? Are you thinking of them?"

She fell back on the divan and covered her eyes with her arm. He heard her breathe as though she were sobbing and leaned over her.

"For God's sake, pull yourself together! Now, Alice, what did I tell you? Do you realize . . . ?"

She revealed her flushed, dry cheeks and sat up furiously, facing him.

"I don't know what you told me! I don't care what you told me! But I do know perfectly well that if you're going to ruin our life together just because once in my existence I slept with a man who wasn't you, I'd rather get out at once! Oh, that'll do . . . !"

She beat the dusty silk cushions with her fists, and her shrill voice became hoarse.

"I feel wretched, Michel; you must understand, you haven't accustomed me to feeling wretched!"

He stood still, bending over her, waiting for her to stop, but didn't seem to hear her any longer.

"Once, you said? You slept with him once? Just once?"

The anxiety that was aging Michel and the childish hope dawning, like the aftermath of a smile, in eyes that she loved, almost made her tell a lie, but she remembered, in time, that she'd talked about three weeks. . . . *He'll remember that too. I know him.* She sat upright, forcing Michel to draw himself up too, and she wiped her forehead, pushing back her black fringe.

"No, Michel. It wasn't an accident; I wasn't taken by surprise. My senses aren't so unpredictable—or so demanding."

He pulled a face and, with a movement of his hand, begged her to stop. Wretchedly he turned away from the overexcited Alice, who looked ugly now, with her untidy hair, because she no doubt resembled the Alice whom another man had conquered. She saw him sitting there with bent head, stripped of his simulated anger and his seductive ways, and quickly invented a way of curing him.

"Listen," she suggested, lowering her voice, "listen to me. What do you want? Naturally you want the truth. Stupidly you want the truth. If I don't tell you the whole truth, as they say, you'll torment us, and what's much worse, you'll become utterly boring about the whole thing."

"Mind what you're saying, Alice!"

She rose, straightened her shoulders and looked her husband up and down.

"But who's listening? What I said is the first part of the truth. Are you going to go on making life miserable for the two of us until you get what you want? Oh, it won't take long! You'll get it. Not later than this evening, when we're alone, when I won't feel that the house . . ." She ended with a glance at the door and walked toward the bedroom.

"Where are you going?" said Michel, out of habit.

She turned around, revealing her ravaged features, her long eyes that had lost their color, her little crushed nose, which was shiny, and her pale mouth.

"You don't think I'm going to let them see me with a face like this?"

"No—I meant, what are you going to do afterwards?"

With her chin she indicated the clear sky and the valley that was visible between the narrow leaves and the sharp-pointed buds.

"I wanted to go over there—to bring back some daffodils . . . to see if there are any lilies of the valley in the Bois Froid. But now . . ."

Her eyelids became swollen and Michel looked away; she seemed so young when she cried that it upset him.

"Wouldn't you like—you don't want me to go with you, naturally?"

She put her hands on his shoulders with a quick gesture that made two round tears fall onto her blue blouse.

"Of course I do, Michel! Come on, Michou! Come on, then; come with me. We'll make the best of it. Come with me. We'll cross the river and go to Saint-Meix to get some eggs. Will you wait for me?"

He replied with a sign, ashamed of his meekness, and collapsed into a chair to wait for her. When she came back, her face powdered and a little *bistre* on her reddened eyelids, her thick hair stretched over her forehead like a silk bandeau, he was asleep, stricken with a sudden, merciful sleep, and didn't even hear her come in.

He slept with his neck awry, his chin crushed against his tie, his expression abnormal and resigned. His empty hands, lying palms upward, quivered slightly. In spite of the short nose and the Roman chin which strengthened the face, he looked like a child grown old, beneath the hair that was tinged with white but grew thickly, and curled if he didn't use hair cream.

Alice leaned over him, held her breath, and was afraid that the old floorboards, which gave way underfoot, might creak. She dared neither wake Michel nor help him to sleep. *Yesterday I would have thrown the old rug over his knees. Or I'd have called out: "Michel, it's such a fine day, come outside! Michel, you're putting on weight!" But today* . . . She tried to feel light-headed again and admitted to herself: *I don't really know the form in a case like mine.*

She turned away, with a vague repugnance, from the closed face, distorted by his posture, and sighed. "To be honest, I've never liked that new little Spanish-type beard." She breathed the words to herself, as though this admission made up a final conclusion and explanation.

She approached the French windows, walking lightly. She felt bored and did not thank Michel for an involuntary truce that interrupted her anxiety and gave her time to think. *Think about what? You don't think before doing something silly; you think afterwards.*

She had the impression that a drop of warm water was running down her spine and turned around with a deep shudder: Michel, awake and motionless, was looking at her! He bore so little resemblance to the poor man she'd seen asleep that she was frightened and went on the defensive.

"What is it?" she asked dully. "Why are you looking at me like that?"

At the sound of Alice's voice, Michel, alert and anxious once again, rose unwillingly.

"I was asleep," he said, passing his hands over his face. "Just imagine, I'd forgotten—"

His tone of excuse displeased Alice, and she cut him short:

"I hadn't. I was waiting. We were supposed to go out."

"Yes. Go out?"

"To Saint-Meix—you know very well."

He sat up again, bestowing a threatening look upon invisible watchers beyond the syringas and the purple lilacs: "Saint-Meix? Fine. I'm coming."

Two hours later, both exhausted, they climbed back up to Cransac, which stood at the top of the slope. The walk had rid them of the desire to exchange the slightest word, and they realized that most of their strength remained back there in the village and a little farther away in the hamlet known as Saint-Meix.

Alice remembered that by the little bridge which linked the Cransac path to the boundary lane, Michel had taken her arm in order to satisfy village curiosity—by presenting a united couple. But as far as the "château" was concerned, did the Cransac people not possess the ferocious flair and vision of beasts of prey?

They noticed that I hadn't changed my shoes; they're covered with dried mud, thought Michel, *and the woman in the chemist's offered Alice cornflower water to bathe her eyelids with. They're terrible.*

Alice remembered, with a sudden feeling of revulsion, that at the Espagnats' Michel had taken hold of her waist and tightened his grip on her arm. Then they had followed the sunny little path to Saint-Meix which wound alongside the high-flowing river, bordered with blue veronica and the flight of cuckoos, illuminated by white hawthorn, where kingfishers and pink-breasted bullfinches flew between the hedges. Beyond the river the first local vineyards grew in reddish, fertile soil, but the wine only began to have any taste higher up, on the pebbly slopes. Every year the short-pruned Cransac vines and the well-tended pathways, which sheltered onions and close-set broad beans, inspired Michel with commonplace ideas about fertility, and lavish gestures which embraced the horizon.

This year he's saying nothing, Alice observed, with a feeling of spite for which she reproached herself.

"There you are, leaves on the vines already!" she cried, in order to arouse her husband's annual enthusiasm.

But he merely let go of Alice's arm and assumed a composed expression again, in which the dignity of an offended husband was tinged with meekness and caution.

"He's an actor, a third-rate actor, like all men," she muttered to herself, her back bent as she climbed the hill on top of which Cransac, a thick, squat country house, with its tiled roofs and small heavy towers, resembled, thought the irreverent Alice, a plump man with his hat pulled too far down.

They stopped at the same time, both out of breath. As a rule Alice showed more resilience than her husband, and was more relaxed, too, beginning to dawdle as the slope became steep, while Michel, out of vanity, went up lightly as though on the attack, almost running, but looking pale, his heart beating unsteadily, all for the traditional pleasure of blurting out a triumphant

"Well?" to Alice when she joined him again. Today the same anxiety undermined both of them, and beneath the foundations of Cransac, purple craggy rocks from which occasional tears of subterranean water flowed, they recovered their breath and made an effort to come closer to each other.

"Not too tired?" asked Michel.

She shook her head in reply, and from the cracks in the rocks she picked fronds of young fern, hardly uncurled, periwinkles growing in the shadow with the blue look of skimmed milk, and the little pink flowers of herb Robert, strong-scented and graceful.

"It's beautiful at this time of day," she said, looking at Cransac above them.

"Yes," he said without enthusiasm.

They set off again at the same pace. *What's in store for me up there?* thought Alice, walking behind Michel, who had taken off his hat. They were feeling the strain because they had taken no rest nor attended to their needs in any way since the morning and felt hot and sticky in their woolen clothes.

At the top of the slope, in the long shadow of the lilac bushes in front of the house, Alice began to walk faster again, but she was halted on the threshold by the question, "Where are you going so fast?" which cut her short. She barely turned, her chin appearing over her shoulder.

"To drink something. I must drink something! I was dying of thirst in that cauldron of a village."

"You could have had a drink down there."

"Lemonade full of flies, and rough cider? No, thanks. Shall I have some water or cider sent out to you on the terrace? That's all I have, apart from apéritifs, black currant, and a bottle of port. Tomorrow—"

She stopped suddenly and fixed her gaze on an invisible point in front of her, but Michel didn't notice the interruption.

"All right, some cider, if you like. Will you come out to the terrace again?"

"Yes. No—not straight away. I can't bear this dress. It's sticking to my back; the wool's rubbing my neck." She finished her sentence with an impatient gesture and disappeared through the arched doorway.

For as long as he could see her he tried hard to make out her figure against the dark vaulted corridor which led to the kitchen, then he sat down on the stone bench with his back to the wall and watched the approach of evening, as green and gentle as twilight in Provence. "You can tell we're near the south . . ."

A nightingale, the nearest one of a band which day and night offered themselves up in song around their well-stocked nests, drowned all the other voices, and Michel began to follow the pattern of the arabesque he was singing, waiting for the return of the long identical notes, each one reinforcing the other. He noted the "*tz-tz-tz,*" which he compared to the sound of rings slipping down over a copper rod, the "*coti-coti-coti*" repeated as many as twenty times without a rest or a pause for breath. He took no pleasure in it, but in testing his breath against the duration of an unending song, he produced a kind of suffocation which prevented him from thinking, and he was aware only of his need to drink.

"Here's the cider," announced Maria. "Will Madame have some too?"

She pulled a cheap metal table alongside the handsome stone bench with its carved feet.

"I don't really know," said Michel. "Madame's changing. Be careful, you clumsy thing. You'll spill all the cider!"

"You're right there," said Maria, full of agreement and approval. "That's me all over!"

With a delicate hand, consisting entirely of bones and tendons, she poured out the cider, so dark in color that even the froth was tinged with yellow, and her small bright eyes sought her master's with a kind of ageless coquetry, so penetrating that Michel shuddered. . . . *How shall we manage to hide anything from Maria?* He felt so weak and defenseless that he was cheered by Alice's return. She was lively and anxious, her face powdered absentmindedly, her nose too white and her mouth too red. But her eyes, always more confident with the approach of evening, which made them look bluer, were wide open, watchful and pale, beneath the black fringe.

"I've put your warm dressing-gown on the bed, Michel," she said from a distance. "The evenings here. . . . And I've put on my thick white flannel, as you can see. Would Maria like something?"

Maria, aware of the indirect question, examined

from top to bottom the long white flannel wrapper and red silk trousers fitting tightly at the ankles. Under her gaze Alice calmly placed her hand on Michel's shoulder.

"I don't want anything," said Maria. "I'm happy as I am."

"Happy about opening the cider bottle badly," muttered Michel. "It doesn't take much to make her happy. What are we eating tonight, Marioućhka?"

"Cabbage soup."

"And then what?"

"Crème caramel. I wanted to make a *daube*, but Madame said—"

"Madame was right," he interrupted. "Be off with you. And serve us on time or I'll cut you out of my will!"

When they were alone Alice tried gently to withdraw her arm. But Michel's head fell violently onto the bend of her elbow, and he held her between his shoulder and cheek, breathing and sighing deeply; his face was warm as he inhaled the familiar scent on her wrist. She freed herself roughly.

"Keep still!" she ordered. "Aren't you ashamed of yourself? Be patient a while, can't you? We'll tell Maria we want to go to bed early."

She didn't dare reveal how far his unreasonable masculine lack of restraint, his jerky sobbing and stammering, left her cold and shocked. Michel overcame his sudden weakness and stood up.

"I'll be back in a moment. Is the water hot enough?"

His quick eyes, gilded by the evening, and by the tears he was holding back, looked enviously at Alice's washed and powdered face, her red and white clothes.

"*They* think it's hot," replied Alice, shrugging her shoulders. "What do *they* know about hot and cold?"

Left alone in her turn she listened to the melody of the nearby nightingale, over a ground bass of distant ones. The former poured out his song with the full voice of a faultless virtuoso, with a splendor and attention to detail that ruled out feeling. But his silences revived the gentle chorus of distant singers, independent and in harmony, close to the females on the nest, disdaining sleep.

Alice hardly relished the green twilight, the redness in the west, above the invisible river. But her solitude, her own silence and the springtime chill, forerunner of the night, restored her strength, along with a kind of impatience which vaguely resembled the anticipation of pleasure. As Michel was late, taking his time, she walked backward and forward on the terrace, which had no balustrade, trying not to shiver, fighting the desire to be cowardly, and everything else, without name or shape, which aided and abetted nervous apprehension.

She could only think of her wrongdoing as a piece of foolishness, inexcusable and unimportant. She was not so much mortified at being taken by surprise and by her clumsiness in lying, as at attempting to avoid the consequences. *It must be sorted out; it must be patched up. There's never been anything like this in our life together!*

And he's decided to be tragic about it! It doesn't suit him to be tragic. She was moving away, with strategic rapidity, from the disastrous moment in the morning which she called "the purple reflection moment," and hastening toward her predestined occupation, her talent as a not overscrupulous repair-worker, hiding, obliterating, forgetting.

A train whistled, then puffed slowly along the valley and stopped at the distant little station. When it started again, balloons of white steam hung for a long time in the motionless air.

Quarter past seven, thought Alice. *If I had caught that train I'd join the express on Laures-Lezières and at two o'clock I'd be in my own place in Paris. That would be silly. A bad evening comes to an end like any other. We shan't be talking about this Ambrogio business forever! Tomorrow, it must be over, or else. . . .*

Michel called her, and she frowned as she saw him looking remarkably fit in his close-fitting vicuna dressing-gown. *Bad sign,* she said to herself. She behaved submissively, and cheerfully urged Maria to serve the cabbage soup.

At table she played Michel's game as well as he did. In the poor light from the chandelier her hair, which she had dampened and smoothed down, gleamed with a wonderfully clear light which changed with the movements of her round head. When she raised her eyes to the old hanging lamp, with its faded frilly shade, her translucent eyeballs became milky-blue, full of the fixed audacity that can be seen in the gaze of the blind. Michel would then stop eating, put his spoon down beside his dish of crème caramel, and wait for Alice to become mellow: to himself he used the word "human."

She's waiting. She's brave; but she won't lose anything by waiting. For nighttime, the return of the moment when, the day before, they had known fulfillment through all their senses, and felt pride in giving and receiving, brought him at last the ferocity which had eluded him all day, and such curiosity that he lost his sense of taste for food and wine.

He watched Alice take two helpings of the crème caramel and heard her say: "Maria has surpassed herself. Congratulations, Maria."

Facing her, Maria's little eyes fixed upon the back of Michel's neck.

"My crème can't be as marvelous as all that. Monsieur hasn't said a word to me."

"Haven't I?" said Michel with a start. "I can't do everything at once, eat and pay you compliments! Must I tell you something, you old horror? Your cabbage soup has made it hard for me to appreciate the caramel. Her soup was like spiced velvet, wasn't it, Alice?"

Since his back was turned to Maria, he allowed himself, as he laughed out loud, to fix an insulting look on his wife. She didn't flinch but folded her napkin and rose, asking, with the gentlest hint of impertinence:

"Coffee?"

Michel's astonishment rewarded her:

"Coffee? What, at night?"

"Haven't you got some work to do after dinner? No? Then will you have a tisane?"

"Tisane, if you'd like some too."

"Yes, I would. Tisane for me too, Maria, please."

While they were dining, a breath of cool air had invaded the library dining room. The first little moths emerged from the tranquil darkness and became prisoners in the lethal areas around the two lamps. Alice straightened the pleated linen lampshade surmounting a pottery vase which had been promoted to artistic lamp. Michel scrutinized the semidarkness and the two top-heavy bookcases whose cornices touched the ceiling.

"Why hasn't Espagnat put a light plug on that side? It looks gloomy. Didn't you tell him to put one in?"

"I can see that he's told tomorrow."

"Oh, tomorrow," he said limply.

Alice turned so quickly that she almost knocked the lamp over.

"What do you mean, 'oh, tomorrow'? Is life going to stop tomorrow? Will the world start turning in the other direction? The house will collapse, we'll be divorced, we won't know each other any longer, will we? Will you say *'Madame'* to me, and shall I call you *'Monsieur'*? Isn't that what you mean by 'oh, tomorrow'? Go on, say it, say it!"

He blinked and stopped himself from flinching beneath this volubility, this terrifying way of attacking, reversing roles, outdistancing everything he'd planned, everything he hadn't had time to plan. Alice stopped of her own accord, listening.

"She's brought the tisane quickly tonight," she murmured. "It usually takes an hour."

She went to meet Maria, opened the rebellious door and held it open. Maria, who was going out quickly, turned on the threshold and asked with feigned timidity, "Madame. It's about the shopping tomorrow morning. Madame hasn't changed her mind at all?"

Alice blew the smoke from her cigarette toward Maria.

"Of course not. Have you forgotten? Braised pigeons and bacon omelet to start with. Is there any problem about the menu?"

"Oh no, Madame. I was just asking. Good night, Monsieur, Madame."

After Maria had gone out, with exaggerated haste and confusion, Alice stretched out her hand toward the closed door.

"Did you see that? You heard what she said! The way she looked around, trying to find evidence! She scents out everything we want to hide! That's where you've landed us."

"What do you mean, that's where . . . Really. Do you know what you've just said? I'd laugh—my goodness yes, I'd laugh—if I could be like you and lose all sense of . . ."

He controlled himself and sat down.

"You're cunning, Alice. I'm well aware of that. Don't worry about Maria. If I let you have your way you'll inundate us with servants' gossip. That's not what I want. You owe me something else tonight."

Her light-colored angry glare met his eyes directly, and he could not make it waver.

"I don't owe you anything. Not that, at least. And, in any case, you must be totally lacking in imagination, like nearly all men, if you're going to ask anything more of me."

Once more he was frightened of this female crudeness of hers; he turned away and took hold of the teapot handle.

"She's broken the lid again," said Alice. "Give it to me. You know very well that the spout pours badly."

He allowed her to fill his cup and put two pieces of sugar in it. So far their customary mutual aid and affectionate foresight remained intact. But Michel was already unhappy; he was hurt that the insolent and guilty Alice should behave, when totally undeserving, just as she had done when innocent. It was too much to think that she was barely affected tonight by the day that was ending, that she looked pretty and was ready for any kind of conflict. However, she collapsed in an instant, sagging completely, when a train rushed out from the hills, cut across the river, whistled and faded away. Standing limply, her cigarette between her fingers, her head lowered, Alice listened to it for a long time.

"So you'd really like to be a long way away, would you?"

She raised her swallowlike head toward him, acknowledging her unwillingness to speak and tell a lie.

She had partly chewed away the lipstick from her broad lower lip, and her eyes, which were turned away from Michel, stared vaguely, beseechingly into the void.

"Yes," she said. "Yes and no. I think I prefer to be here all the same. Where would I go?"

"You say that now!" he cried out in constrained tones. "That's all right now! You should have thought of that before going off to bed with that—that half-wit! But when you want to do something, my goodness . . ."

She shrugged her shoulders.

"Stupid. Oh yes, you're stupid. Anyone might think you didn't know me. Going off to bed. You've really spelled it out, the thing you're really afraid of. That's just how I behave, isn't it, picking up men whenever I feel like it!"

"Not quite, but you've done it once. While I was slaving away down there—"

"Michel," she interrupted condescendingly, "admit that you've taken on work that was more exhausting, and more successful, too, than running a miserable little pink plaster place for two months, on behalf of the Schmil brothers. I'd already told you so: 'Michel, it's a waste of time. It's a winter thrown away. The Schmil brothers aren't lucky like Moyses.' A woman can sense luck better than a man can."

He listened, and her words threw him off course.

Impatiently he unfastened his dressing-gown; Alice recognized the pajamas that he had worn the preceding night, one of the light cigar-colored pairs that he chose because they matched the color of his eyes. She saw too the small teeth that he looked after with creditable vanity, and the hands he was proud of; she breathed in a scent which she usually described as being "light brown" too, and suddenly felt wildly possessive. *He's my property; this man belongs to me; am I stupidly going to throw everything away, through his fault and mine?* "Let's get on with it," she said suddenly.

She went to the window to throw away her cigarette end, with one of those actions which men call masculine, came back to light another, and sat down comfortably in the armchair that flanked the bureau. She was conscious of her own free movements, deliberately choosing the cane chair, with the table as an arm rest, and accepting the light from the lamp on her face, while generously leaving to Michel the divan and the semidarkness. The waxing moon filled the long uncurtained window with powdery blue light, while the pink glow from the lamp reached the nearest stars on the syringa.

"Another cup of tisane, Michel?"

"No, will you stop being so nice to me? That's enough."

From the clear-cut, overgentle voice that came from the shadow, she assumed that things could not be put off any longer.

"Don't you remember that I had flu while you were at Saint-Raphaël?"

"Yes, I remember very well. If you hadn't had flu you'd have come with me."

"That's right. I didn't want to bore you with my flu, even in my letters."

"Precisely. And I know now that you had other things to do."

Impetuously she swept away the cigarette ash that had just fallen on the table.

"None of that, Michel! Make your 'cruel allusions' and other witty remarks some other time. Just now, I'm talking—or I'm not talking. Stop being sarcastic, will you?"

In the protection of the darkness, he received the nearsighted blue gaze that was blazing through the tight eyelashes, full of insolent courage. *She's never looked so much like an Annamite with fair skin.*

"Very well," he said laconically, "I'm listening."

At first she seemed embarrassed by his acquiescence and faltered as she began.

"Yes. . . . You must remember that I wasn't at my best. When *Ladies for the Gentlemen* went on tour, you'd left me to deal with everything—which I did—while you put on that rotten season at Saint-Raphaël. So it's not surprising if flu . . ."

In the darkness he wasn't really listening to her. As she spoke, his fatigue and the novelty of a floating unhappiness which didn't yet know where to settle took Michel unexpectedly back to Alice's youth and his own, to a time when Alice's life was full of risks; she belonged to a family overwhelmed with daughters who knew they were a burden and struggled furiously to make a living. One of Alice's sisters played the violin in a cinema in the evenings, while another was a mannequin with Lelong and lived on black coffee. Alice drew, cut out dresses, and sold a few ideas for interior decoration and furnishing. "The Four Arts," as they were called, formed a mediocre string quartet with piano and played in a big brasserie that went bankrupt. A little box-office window framed the beautiful head and torso of Hermine, the eldest, when Michel became director of the Théâtre de l'Etoile. But he loved only the least pretty of these four lively, ingenious girls, who were elegant in their poverty and devoid of humility. *If I'd been crazy about Colombe or Bizoute, would the same thing have happened?* At the sound of Alice's minor-key voice he was dreaming, strangely free of anxiety, convinced he would be brought back to the present when she came to the worst. *Oh,* he sighed to himself, *let's get on to the deluge . . .*

"You remember too that you'd told Ambrogio to do nothing without consulting me, and not even to let a line of publicity appear without talking to me, and without my telephoning you at midnight."

Ambrogio! he thought with a start. *Yes, Ambrogio! How is it that I've thought so little about him since this morning? Ambrogio. . . .*

He didn't want to interrupt Alice, but did so in spite of himself:

"Talking to you, talking to you. . . . What about the telephone?"

She forced herself to speak in a careful, precise manner, sometimes gazing down at the cigarette she was stubbing out, sometimes seeking Michel's face beyond the lamp.

"Precisely," she said. "The telephone. It was one day

when Ambrogio hardly recognized my voice over the telephone—I'd had my throat cauterized that morning. He was worried, and in the afternoon . . ."

She improvised without effort, carried along by the comforting rhythm of ordinary lying. *It's not the whole truth*, she recognized within herself, *but it's the next best thing.*

". . . And it's when he saw the state I was in that he said to me: 'What, you haven't written to Arbezat that you had a temperature of 38.8? It's ridiculous! Don't bother about anything! There's so little to do here, I'll take care of everything. I'll report every day on the takings at l'Etoile, and the rehearsals for *The Golden Scarab*.' . . . What?"

"I didn't say anything," said Michel.

"Oh, I thought . . . Do you understand the situation?"

"Very clearly," said Michel. "Your convalescence. Your bedroom which is always too hot, and the pink sheets. You were weak; you looked sleepy like an Indochinese girl who's been smoking too much. That man from Nice bringing you flowers and talking finance to the tune of 'My Kiss Can Bite.' "

He had a coughing spasm and had to get up to drink some tepid tisane, then went back to his divan. Alice had time to see that his expression was confused and uncertain and his eyes bloodshot.

"Go on. I'm listening."

She took the time to drink something, too, while reflecting quickly and clearly. In the silent countryside the loud-voiced nightingale was embarking once more on his night of trills, full fluted notes, variations of infinite range and isolated sounds which imitated the fallen pearl of some amorous toad. *He can hear it too,* thought Alice. *He's thinking about it. He's thinking about last night. Careful.*

She plucked up courage again like a tired, cautious swimmer.

"Well, no," she said. "It wasn't at all like that. Not at all. I myself could easily have thought . . . what you're thinking. But that boy—"

She lingered over her sentence to make sure that Michel tolerated her way of referring to Ambrogio.

"That boy, as I came to know him better, appeared quite different from what I'd supposed. Yes, just imagine. More . . . more *subtle,* spending his time differently from the way one might have thought; more . . . better acquainted with a whole lot of things that used to interest me. He's musical. So we talked a lot. What?"

"I didn't say anything," said Michel. "I laughed."

She looked sadly at the face she could hardly see.

"Michel, I beg you. I'm doing all I can; try to be sincere too, and straightforward; don't make it impossible for me to do what you've asked; I'm trying to do it. You've been ill, you know what convalescence is like; it's a kind of—indecision; people get desperately tired for no reason; they need trust and help."

In the darkness she saw him raising his slender hand and she broke off.

"I prefer," he said, raising his voice slightly, "I distinctly prefer you not to talk to me about your convalescence. Leave it. Describe the rest. Only the rest."

She returned the stroke with the ease of a good player.

"But there's nothing more to describe!" she cried. "Will you force me to tell, down to the last detail, how giving way to a man is the end of a very long conversation, the climax of the excitement that comes from having a temperature, that comes because it's late . . . it's the proof—superfluous, oh yes, and even out of place—the proof of the trust and friendship you've just exchanged, and after that you don't want to hold anything back."

It was very painful to her; her cheekbones and eyes were red. She got up, dropped her hands alongside her thighs and complained aloud:

"It's shameful what you're asking me. Shameful. And it doesn't help, it doesn't solve anything. The reverse, in fact. If you think that deep down inside I can forgive you that . . . I suppose you're satisfied now."

She opened the French window wide and breathed in the springtime night, so perfect, so full of luxurious scents hanging in the still air, intangible humidity, moonlight and song, that angry tears came to her eyes. "It's too silly. A night like this! Spoiling a night like this, when we're still quite capable of staying out on the bench and wrapping ourselves up to watch the progress of the stars and the moon going down."

She suddenly valued at their true price the late season of love, the modest hours when a loving attachment, lying deeply submerged, is at rest, and she turned around to rescue everything that was in danger of death. At the same time she became aware of Michel's silence. He was still there, half-lying, leaning on one elbow.

"Michel?"

"Yes."

"What's the matter?"

"Nothing."

She lost heart and sat down.

"Will you tell me what you're thinking? You forced me to talk. Can we hope for peace and a quiet life?"

"Oh," he said disparagingly, "you haven't told me very much—apart from the worst."

"What do you mean, the worst?"

He jumped up, and as he came into the area of light his features looked changed and shrunken.

"The worst. You don't even understand that the worst is precisely the—the friendship you showed the chap, those hours when you talked to each other, before going to bed together. You even uttered the word 'trust,' my goodness. You said he liked the things you like—"

"I'm sorry, you mustn't confuse—I haven't made myself clear."

"Be quiet!" he shouted at the top of his voice, banging his fists down on the bureau close to Alice. The shouting and the gesture seemed to calm him. Alice barely concealed her approval. *It's high time he raised his voice. If he goes on like that, we'll probably understand each other.* Slightly too late, she drew back, as though afraid, and folded her raised arms over her face.

But he was already moving away and regaining his moderation.

"My poor child. You'll never understand what it's like to be a man in love, nor how a man reacts to treachery. You'll never understand that a man can forgive a woman for going to bed with someone else, that he can almost forget about a brief physical attraction . . ."

"And so he should," she said drily.

He looked her in the face, fully aware of his rights as a man of swift desires.

"And so he should, precisely."

He walked up and down, his hands in the pockets of his open dressing-gown, shrugging his shoulders like a man with broad-minded views.

"Surprised. Intoxicated. A nasty moment of excitement. For God's sake, we know what it's like, we men. Let him cast the first stone, if he's got the courage, the man who . . ."

She looked at him and listened silently, now angry once again. *The funniest thing of all is that he believes it; he thinks he knows what a woman's desire is like.* She allowed herself a silent laugh, while he plunged into the darkness between the two bookcases.

He came close to her again and seized hold of her arms above the elbows.

"But, my poor child, you'd have told me: 'One evening, you see, just as it was getting dark, I lost my head, rather. There was something in the air . . .' But I'd have been the first to understand and forgive, my poor child."

She freed herself violently. "If you call me your poor child again I'll throw the teapot at you!" she cried. "No, don't ask me why, or I'll make a scene!"

She felt exhausted, incapable of starting a fight again and keeping it up.

"I'm going to bed," she said faintly. "To bed—I'm going to bed. You can't offer me anything as attractive as that. I'm going to bed. Good night."

She went out, her red scarf trailing from one hand along the floor, like an empty net.

When he made up his mind to go to the bedroom, Alice seemed to be asleep. She had turned toward the wall, and between her dark hair and the sheet, which came up to her mouth, Michel could make out only the gently curving line of her lowered eyelids and her strange nostrils. She breathed silently. The gray-green of her eyes belonged to the West, but when she closed them her entire face had a look of the Far East.

As his body touched the cool sheets Michel began to shiver nervously and realized what a long hour he had spent alone on the divan, now streaked with moonlight. He had contemplated sleeping in the library, in spite of the mouse and the bodies of insects tapping against the window. Now that he was in bed he resolved to bear his suffering without moving. But his unhappiness lacked rhythm, virtuoso quality and plan. His torment constantly eluded him, and trifling everyday worries took its place. *I intended to ask Willemetz to lend me Candelaire for a casino tour. I haven't written to Ambrogio to hold up the printing of the programs for the Etoile.* He suddenly remembered that the mayor of Cransac was expecting him to luncheon in two days, and his heart jumped painfully.

Once the lamp was out, the moonlight shone into the room over the top of the venetian blinds, forming the shape of a harp. Michel turned toward Alice's bed. *Is she really asleep? It seems incredible.* He didn't trust the immobility of her body; she lay on her side, her knees drawn up, a faint aura of perfume surrounding her, and she was so close that he could have touched her. He knew from much enjoyable experience that Alice could remain motionless for nights on end. At times when their love had sought out all types of pleasurable renunciation, Michel could keep his young wife lying lightly beside him, all night, and although her eyes were closed he was never sure whether she was asleep or not. . . . *Can she really be sleeping after a day like this?*

He thought he was suffering, but for the time being he was merely uneasy, uncomfortable and stiff. He felt between his ribs for a spot where his vague pain might come to a head and establish itself. He took care not to move in the hope of avoiding the surprisingly loud noise made by a naked body between the rise and fall of sheets in the stillness of night. He carried his worries into his sleep and perpetually dreamed that he was awake, so that he never discovered whether Alice had pretended to be asleep or not.

For when he opened his eyes he was greeted by an empty bed and the distinct sound of a high-pitched voice which came from the window and was not addressed to him.

"Yes, Chevestre, we're lazy! Half past eight, Chevestre, and my husband's still asleep, just imagine! What have you got to tell us, Chevestre? Good news, as usual?"

Michel awoke with his mind a blank, light-hearted except for some vague undefined worry which was flying toward him from a great distance. He thought at first that this worry was identified with his agent.

She's making a mistake, he thought, *she shouldn't joke with Chevestre. His sense of humor's restricted to playing me dirty tricks, as he did over that mortgage business, for example.*

"Alice!" he called out in a low voice. She let go of the window frame and turned around. She was all in blue, a full-length garment of faded shantung which she called her charlady's overall. Then he realized his mistake. The worry and illness that tormented him, the pain between his ribs which made it difficult to breathe —it was this tall blue woman, her blue so soft and washed out, as blue as the moist patch of sky between two clouds, where the first star rises after a shower.

"Are you awake?"

She brought back into the room a little of the laughter she had just directed outside, the bantering disdain she kept for Chevestre. At first Michel didn't see her swollen eyes; he noticed only the insolent youthfulness of her body and her movements, her silky head and her powdered face.

"It's Chevestre," she told him meaningfully, as though she'd said, "Don't appear in the nude."

He replied merely with an angry gesture, motioning her to close the window. She did nothing of the sort and went on in the same way:

"Breakfast's ready, Michel. No, Chevestre, don't wait for my husband; we're dying of hunger. You can find him this afternoon, or before lunch; we're not likely to be going out. Fine, Chevestre, we'll see you later."

Michel got up and gropingly tightened his pajama cord, looked around for his morning glass of water and smoothed back his hair, turning his face away from the full daylight.

"I was just going to get you up, Michel. It's such a wonderful day that I've had breakfast served on the terrace. Maria nearly had a fit. There's some honey from the bees they found under the roof. It's rather dark but very good. Be quick."

She went out rapidly, her bare feet in moccasins, leaving him limp and vague, obsessed by the need to obey his wife, something he always did in matters of eating, drinking and taking care of himself. He combed his hair and pressed his lips together in order to tighten up his cheeks and make them look younger. Then he looked carefully at his bloodshot eyes: *There's only six years between us; how does she manage to look like a young woman?*

He went out of the house looking like a man summoned to appear in court, his face so artificially composed that Alice, who was seated some way off at the table, looked at him in amazement. But she suppressed her astonishment and turned the handles of the coffeepot and milk jug toward her husband.

"Did you sleep well?" she inquired.

"I slept."

The shadow of a catalpa, with its flower-laden leafless branches, lay across the tablecloth. A torpid bee flew clumsily toward the honey pot, and Michel waved his napkin to drive it away. But Alice held out her long slim hand to protect the bee.

"Leave her alone! She's hungry. And she's working."

Her eyes suddenly filled with tears. Michel saw them quivering on the broad irises, the silver-gray color of a willow tree. *What a life,* he thought vindictively. *Every time we open our mouths we come up against some concealment, some sensitive wound. What's she breaking her heart over now? Is it that drowsy bee, the word hunger, or the word work?*

Alice had already overcome her weakness; she was spreading butter and dark honey on the rough country bread. "Wonderful weather!" she cried. But Michel, feeling the cold, pulled his dressing-gown tightly over his chest and added that the air was as cool as peppermint. The first mouthful he ate and his first taste of hot coffee restored a little of his physical well-being, which he concealed by knitting his brows and refusing to see round about him the blue morning dew, the clear pale sky, and the periwinkle flowers and May tree which looked slightly mauve in the shadow. Alice spoke quietly, trying to make him feel better.

"Look. All the white things seem almost blue. Have you noticed that the swallows are coming back to their old nests? Can you feel how hot the sun is? You can have some more milk, you know. I've arranged to have two litres a day—an orgy."

He nodded, but protested silently, calling himself to witness: *Look at her, the minx. She's making a virtue out of everything. The air, the May tree, the coffee. Everything helps her to forget. If only I could let go.* He had just raised to his lips the first cigarette of the day, the best one, but he lowered his hand limply and closed his eyes: *If only I could let go,* he sighed. *Oh, how happy I could still be!*

The telephone bell rang unsteadily inside the house, and Maria, austerely neat and tidy in her black dress, white cap and apron, appeared at the door.

"Telephone for Monsieur!" she cried. "It's Paris!"

Michel put down his napkin and went inside without looking at his wife. As soon as she was alone, she stopped smoothing down the butter in the dish, replacing the lid on the sugar bowl, and protecting the honey from the ants with a glass plate. She froze to attention. But Michel had closed the heavy old nail-studded door behind him. She sat there motionless, her lower lip drooping, her neck stretched forward. She had the equivocal look of some guilty Tonkinese, and her expression changed only when she heard Michel saying in a louder and quite friendly voice:

"That's it, then, isn't it: no concession beyond the agreed figure? Fine. Good-bye, old chap. Thank you. Good-bye!"

He came back with a casual air and sat down without saying a word, gazing into the distance. Alice tried to find some sign of reassurance, but he didn't help her.

"Was it . . . ?"

"Paris," he said, exhaling smoke.

"I know that!"

"Then why ask?"

"Was it— It couldn't have been Ambrogio? I heard you saying 'Thank you. Good-bye, old chap.' "

Since this prevented him from lying, he defied her.

"On the contrary, it was Ambrogio. Who else could it have been?"

In her surprise she hesitated, and he thought she was upset.

"I said what I had to say," replied Michel firmly. "He was talking business, as he should. I gave him my instructions."

She looked at him in astonishment, closely examining his mouth, his eyes, his curly hair with its white streaks, and his bronze silk cravat, as though Michel had emerged from a cellar full of cobwebs. He shook off the penetrating gray-green look with a quick retort:

"Well? Did you expect anything else?"

"What? No. Obviously not. May I take the tray in? Maria has to go down to the village."

She sounded confused, and hurried off with the tray as though it had suddenly begun to rain. *He said "thank you" to him; he called him "old chap"; he said "good-bye."*

In the kitchen she broke a cup and cut herself slightly at the base of her thumb. She sucked her hand, which was trembling, and relished the salty taste of her blood and its color, as though it were some cordial which no other creature could provide for her. She leaned against the kitchen door, pressing her hand to her mouth and repeating the words of malediction: *He called him "old chap"; he said "thank you" to him.*

They survived their second morning fairly easily by keeping a grip on themselves, and sat down to table as though they were past masters in the art of eating lunch. Alice persuaded her husband that he really should go to see the mayor before the little banquet that was fixed for the next day; she discoursed upon the links that united Cransac the village and Cransac the manor, and also upon the importance of good neighborly relations. Michel agreed, pretending to forget that whenever he concerned himself with his native Cransac, Alice paraded her bohemian indifference, retreating shortsightedly behind a veil of cigarette smoke. But Maria opened her eyes, which were as black and golden as secret little mountain streams, those miserly springs deep down in the little slaty hollows. For the first time she admired Alice, and as a sign of approval she thrust out her forehead, as young oxen do when new to the yoke.

Behind the half-closed shutters the dining room smelled as usual of slightly acid fruit and a well-polished confessional. A ray of sunlight fell across the table, lighting up their hands as they held the dishes and broke up the bread. Alice thought her husband looked frivolous, with his raised little finger, while Michel watched the movements of Alice's long nimble hands, the long-fingered hand which had written to Ambrogio, which had opened to Ambrogio a door whose hinges made no sound . . . the hand which had lingered, now tense, now sleepy and relaxed, in a man's hair, while the two of them whispered terrible, secret words. From his shadowy river bank he eyed the hands with the light playing over them and screwed up his eyes like a patient angler, but never forgot a single line his role required of him.

"And then," suggested Alice, "while you're with the mayor, you could have the car cleaned at Brouche's garage."

"Really! Fancy starting to keep the car clean! Wild extravagance! Couldn't that husband of yours clean the car, Maria?"

Maria put her teaklike hands together and gazed heavenward.

"My husband? You talk as though you didn't know what he's like! It makes no difference whether he's around or not, I'm the only one who ever does anything."

Michel raised his carefully manicured hand and then brought it down again on the table.

"Did you hear what she said, Alice? She's so funny!"

"She's not funny," said Alice. "She knows what men are like."

A plate escaped Maria's grasp, and Alice thought she could see a dark flush rising to the roots of her hair. The servant apologized in her fine southern speech:

"You see, you upset me, Madame . . ."

"Break another forty like that," joked Michel, "and you've got a future on the music-hall stage."

"It's no laughing matter. It could have been a very valuable plate," said Maria in severe reproach. "Isn't that so, Madame?"

"We haven't got any very valuable plates here, Maria. Bring us the coffee quickly. I think Monsieur is in rather a hurry."

"What's the matter with her?" asked Michel when they were alone. "The old girl's off form. First of all she breaks a plate, and then she scolds me. And how did you get the impression I'm in a hurry? I've only got tedious things to do at Cransac."

He was grumbling, and Alice listened to his complaining like some child who'd been unfairly punished. *He noticed something too. Maria went against him. A hint of criticism. In fact, I think she sometimes finds him a bit common. . . .*

She saw her husband leave, waved to him and then reproached herself for doing so. *I think I'm going too far. I'm not very sure now how we should behave toward each other. If I worked things out my way, what would I do?* She raised her head and questioned the air about her, which hummed with the sound of a distant swarm of bees, a faint throbbing which seemed to be the feverish pulse of spring. The reddish-colored soil was drenched with recent rain, and as the surface dried it turned pink. Beyond a stretch of meadow and the dense wood there was no longer any white mist indicating the invisible river.

What would I do? He'll telephone to Ambrogio again tomorrow, and every day after that. Should I warn Ambrogio? Oh, no, never!

Unconsciously she began to feel prudish. *I'm not in touch with Ambrogio! And then, it doesn't matter if I despise Michel, but as for that silly man Ambrogio knowing how—how patient Michel is, no, he mustn't!*

A sudden intolerance made her walk down toward the syringas at the end of the terrace and sniff them. But the syringa was awaiting evening before exuding its scent. Alice turned back one sleeve, offering her white-skinned arm to the bite of the April sunshine, and reached up to the crabapple tree with its red and pink flowers. *Those three beautiful branches in the gray vase.* But she lost enthusiasm, let go of the branch and allowed the flowers to live. *And we've only got as far as the second day. I was braver yesterday. But yesterday he hadn't spoken to Ambrogio on the telephone and called him "old chap."*

She tried to pull herself together and see the thing honestly. *I really don't want them to come to blows or send each other seconds over something that's so . . .* She tried to find the word, but could only think of "futile!"—didn't even feel like smiling, and gave up there and then her attempted impartiality. She decided not to polish the taps in the bathroom, not to measure the dining room windows for curtains. It was prudence rather than laziness that made her stop at the doorway to the house, gauging the length of the noonday shadow in the vestibule, and she went back to the terrace without admitting to herself that this deep shadow, advancing over the flagstones, made her just a little frightened today.

Before, I wasn't frightened. Before, I would have taken the short cut and waited for Michel at the crossroads. I'd have got into the car and we'd have gone to Sarzat-le-Haut to see the view. But today . . .

She went to get the leather blotter, which she handled without resentment, and placed it on the iron table, facing the handsome carved stone bench. *Suppose I write to Bizoute?* It wasn't that she preferred Bizoute to Hermine, or Hermine to Colombe. Bizoute passed on to Colombe, or Hermine, the few letters she received from Alice—four, six or ten pages of unimportant news, jokes that went back to adolescence.

"My dear Bizoute,

Just imagine, you three, I'm writing this outside. I've no stockings on; it's just like August . . ."

Between Cransac and Alice came the vision of a little studio apartment in Vaugirard, rather poor, cheerful, badly furnished. As she wrote she felt she could touch the baby grand piano which jutted out across the doorway, and the trestle table laden with manuscript music paper; she inhaled the familiar smell of tobacco and inexpensive jasmine perfume. Was the black enameled plate still there, full of cigarette ends, moved about from the piano to the table, from the table to the arm of the big easy chair? She smiled across the hills of Cransac toward the old house in Paris, took refuge in the elusive pleasure of remembering the close-knit fraternity, the physical and mental resemblance, daring but innocent, which united the four daughters of old Eudes, who taught Solfeggio and the piano. They'd been as close as twin sisters, as affectionate as animals must be when born the same day, to the same mother; they enjoyed struggling together, they had a frantic desire not to die of hunger or disease, they shared all they possessed and all they lacked—two hats for the four of them, dresses without underwear, scanty meals which Bizoute described as "the Hollywood diet."

Alice contemplated her vanished youth with cautious and sober regret. Was she risking a return to the uncomfortable warm studio apartment, its walls stained yellow with sunshine and cigarette smoke, hearing once more the sound of the piano at which Hermine and Bizoute, composers destined to perpetual obscurity, would sit with cigarettes dangling from their lips, leaning on each other's shoulders, their eyes half-closed, trying to devise orchestral themes and songs for some film?

A flower from the catalpa spun round in the air and fell on the letter Alice had begun, across the vivid picture of the piano that was too big for the room and the revolving piano stool. ". . . just like August. Michel is playing the château-owner in town. I'm taking advantage of his absence to relax with the three of you on our native toutounier. How is the *tricbalous?* And is the *brédédé-à-roulettes* still *antibouenne?*"

She felt ashamed and stopped. *Is that all I can find to say to them? Those silly old jokes from our teenage days, those—* But she knew that Bizoute would laugh as usual, and would read with secret compunction those passwords which protected an inviolate period of their existence from all outsiders. Hermine would probe the air with the tips of her invisible antennae, cough out her smoke, and reply through space, like shepherds who sing out from hill to hill in their solitude: "The *brédédé-à-roulettes* has reduced its rates of pay yet again: one hundred and fifty francs for a song entitled 'Just a Little Higher,' one of those delicate creations which edify the soul, and in which we specialize. As for the *tricbalou,* I must admit he's a real *balabi,* or, to make myself quite clear, a *zog* of the first water. Don't worry about the Marquise de Joinville; work's started in the studios again. She's still a film editor, and on top of that our Colombe Noire isn't worried about money. If you go to see the production of *Her Majesty Mimi*—a minor masterpiece of humor and sentiment—watch carefully the scene where Mimi reviews her army: the third horse from the right is our beloved sister . . ."

The freshening breeze from the east began to flutter through the writing pad which Alice was covering with her uneven, flexible handwriting, small at the margins and big as she started each new page. From time to time she would stop to watch the blue of evening rise, flow and deepen between the folds of the hills. But over the cherry blossoms that still looked white and the last flowers on the peach trees floating alongside the vines, she tried to see only one thing: the warm little studio, the two tall girls, their looks a little faded now, slightly tired of laughing and working together. Love occupied only a small discreet place in their lives, for one sister remained faithful to a conductor who was married, while the other was mysteriously involved with a person whose name she never revealed—the others called him "Monsieur Weekend." *And suppose it was Madame Weekend! That would be odd,* thought Alice gaily. Then the Dauphine landscape once more shut out the Vaugirard home, and she became gloomy.

When I think about my family as much as that, it's because I'm finding Michel terribly boring. I know myself too well. . . . I can hear the car. Is he back already?

A moment later Michel jumped out of the car, straight-backed and light of foot. *He's definitely a good-looking man. I've always thought those hazel eyes were most attractive. All the same, I didn't enjoy seeing him again.* As she watched him approach she felt suddenly frigid, in a ruthless, feminine way. But Michel spoke to her from some distance away, and at the sound of his voice she suddenly melted.

"Can you tell me—can you tell me if this is what Maria asked me to get? It's—it's something ending in ol—oh, were you writing a letter?"

"Yes, to Bizoute. I haven't finished it yet, but it's not important; it can go tomorrow." *My goodness, he must think I'm writing to warn my crazy lover of last year. Yes, look at the purple blotter, my poor Michel, yes. . . . What a strange look on his face! Oh yes, the purple blotter's got the plague; it stinks. . . .*

Without a word she placed a reassuring hand on Michel's shoulder.

"Are you laughing about something?" he said in a low voice.

"No, I'm not laughing."

"But you want to laugh."

She slapped her thighs: "Have I made a vow that I'd never laugh again? Michel, Michel, don't behave like an old bear! You're back, I'm glad to see you back, I didn't expect you so soon. I know I'm beyond the pale, but let me be cheerful for a moment; let me turn somersaults and blow bubbles in my own disgusting mud."

"Be careful," he interrupted her in the same low, urgent voice. "Get into the habit of being careful. Yes, I'm back early. I've seen my people."

"Your people?"

"The mayor, Ferreyrou; I've settled it."

"Settled what?"

"I'm not going down there to lunch tomorrow. I told them I'd got here from Paris in poor shape. I couldn't go to a banquet in Cransac and just drink mineral water, so we'd better put it off. Does that annoy you, then? In the end I told them I was ill."

He leaned on the iron table with both hands and closed his eyes. His face looked drained. Alice could see wrinkles; he had the pallor of a city dweller, while his mouth and forehead had grown old in twenty-four hours.

"Very well," she said at once. "Let's be invalids! That suits me perfectly. Dressing-gowns at all hours of the day, mulled wine at six o'clock, and we shan't go beyond what remains of the boundary wall!"

"But won't you be bored?"

"I'm sure I will! It's an excellent idea. Any more parcels? Give them to me and put the car away. No, wait, I'll put it away myself. Stand back! You'll see some splendid reversing!"

"No, no!" cried Michel. "Get out, for heaven's sake! You can have anything you want, if only you'll get out! My power of attorney! My cross of Isabella the Catholic. The right mudguard's touching! Hard around, hard around!"

He jumped onto the runningboard while she handled the car like a beginner, albeit swearing like an experienced driver. They came back from the garage feeling hot but pleased with themselves. Michel's face clouded only when he saw the lean figure of Chevestre walking slowly toward the terrace. He was dressed in deferential black, wearing tight well-polished leggings which from a distance looked like boots.

"There he is," said Michel in a low voice. "It's for me to say when he can wear boots."

"I thought you were expecting him."

"I was, yes. But when I expect him I always hope he won't come. It annoys me, the way he looks as though he's going to take over."

He admitted only his annoyance and concealed as well as he could that classic fear felt by every landowner when faced by his agent. After rising from odd-job man to farmer, Chevestre had exchanged his soft cap for an old felt hat and looked smart in a jacket. Whenever they were alone together Michel, feeling humiliated by Chevestre's awkward, heronlike bearing, would try in vain to use his polite business approach and the bluff manner he had learned from realistic plays.

The wiry Chevestre came closer; his clipped fair moustache, which was turning white, cut across his face like a piece of tow. *He's the man who put up the money for the mortgage on Cransac,* thought Michel. *Seysset only gave his name. If Alice knew. . . . She'll know when I have to sell.* Alice too was watching Chevestre carefully as he walked up toward them.

"You know, Michel, your agent's got something. He's a bastard, but there's an air about him."

After ten years Alice still hasn't learned to say "our agent." She doesn't belong here. She never will. Does she realize that? But she doesn't really care. She's going to put Chevestre on his guard by asking leading questions; she's going to raise her voice when she wonders why the osiers have split, and she'll advise giving quince jelly to cure the chickens' dysentery. She doesn't realize how much people dislike her artistic manner.

"Do you want me to stay?" asked Alice. "Chevestre doesn't bother me at all."

"Nor me. I'll see you in the library. But don't look as though you're dashing off without saying good morning. He's here now. Chevestre," he called out, "must I force you to join me for a glass of port?"

"Oh no, sir, oh no. But work's like a pretty woman: it won't wait."

Chevestre removed the hat from his cropped head and waited deferentially for Alice to move in his direction. She did not hurry unduly, offering him first her long hand and then a packet of cigarettes. She peered closely into Chevestre's blue eyes and asked what the weather would be like the next day, while Michel, displaying his country-gentleman smile, felt angry that the meeting between Alice and his agent resembled that of a well-bred man and an attractive woman.

"What did he tell you, in fact?"

"Nothing. Well, nothing new. He manages to put forward various possibilities in such a smooth, airy-fairy way that when you try to sum up and pinpoint what he's suggested, he opens his eyes wide: 'But I never said to Monsieur. . . . But it never occurred to me. . . . Michel knows very well that I just couldn't afford—' "

"What couldn't he afford?"

Michel shrugged his shoulders and lied.

"How do I know! Don't assume that Chevestre's the

sort of man who'd give away his plans, if he's got any! And I must admit that I can't really concentrate on what he's saying, just now."

"Why not? Oh, I see," she said thoughtlessly.

"Alice!"

She refrained from making an irrelevant reply and tried once again to distract Michel from his worry.

"Why does he talk to you in the third person?"

"His father worked for our neighbors the Capdenacs as a valet."

"Oh really? I felt he was one of those awkward fair-haired Frenchmen with a long tradition behind him. But he can't be. I was convinced his father was a former officer of the hussars and his mother a sheaf of corn."

She spoke idly, trying to be amusing, while walking up and down in order to escape her husband's attention.

"The weather's changing; the east wind's getting up. As someone I know would say, 'They'll have the mistral in Nice tonight.' Oh! Wait a minute!"

She ran over to the woodshed and came back with small sticks of firewood, pine cones and beechwood chips, with which she lit a bright fire.

"Because we've had two wonderful days, we think it's summer, and then— Now wasn't this a good idea?"

She turned around proudly. The firelight shone golden in Michel's eyes as he gazed fixedly on the flames.

"Michel . . ."

Sitting down on the stone flags by the hearth, she

made herself sound plaintive and youthful, testing out the power of the voice he loved.

"What did I say just now—what were we going to do? Oh yes, the mulled wine."

Michel stood up to close the door which constantly came open, and, looking along the wall, she followed the slow-moving shadow of a broad-shouldered man with a round curly head, a shadow she felt she was seeing for the first time.

"Don't close the door. I'm going to the kitchen to arrange for the mulled wine. Are you tired, Michel?"

"Yes, I'm tired," he said absentmindedly. "I'm not feeling too good." He looked at the sky with its flying clouds, and the young leaves, flattened by the wind like weeds in a stream. "I think the weather's really taken a turn for the worse," he added. "And the barometer —oh dear, the barometer!"

He turned around as the door slammed. Alice was hurrying to the kitchen, escaping from Michel, his talk about the weather and the leaden afternoon light. In the warm kitchen, where the walls were hung with brightly polished copper, she uttered a sigh of relief.

"My goodness, that smells good! What is it, Maria?"

"The guinea fowl, Madame. I started it early; like that it won't sit on the dish too long; it'll all disappear! Madame would like the mulled wine? Get up, you ill-mannered thing! Go and get the red wine at once!"

Maria's witchlike arm sent her husband out of the kitchen. Two slow-moving sabots, a rough corduroy jacket stained with earth, and a powerful, despondent back were banished. Alice sat down for a moment on the chair he had vacated. *How cozy it is! Food cooking slowly, the stove red-hot, it's so warm I feel dizzy. This thin little grasshopper organizing that pathetic man. How human it all is, so normal and pleasant! And if the servant doesn't care for me, that's normal too. I'd like to stay here.*

Maria's silence forced her to her feet.

"Maria, don't forget the cinnamon in the mulled wine, and the eight lumps of sugar."

She went straight through the library dining room, where Michel was writing a letter, and lingered in the bathroom. With the help of the warm wine, and the dinner that followed, with the guinea fowl melting in their mouths, they put a brave face on things. Once it had turned half past nine, Alice called Maria back twice, asking her to put a hot-water bottle in her bed and later to find an eiderdown. Then Michel and Alice remained alone and heard the muffled chimes of ten o'clock from the little clock that stood high up, just below the ceiling, on a thuja-wood base. Michel smoked as he finished his letters, while Alice sat down in the least uncomfortable of the armchairs and opened the previous day's newspapers. Otherwise it might have looked as though she were reading her present and her future in the fire. *Ten o'clock. If we were in Paris . . .*

"Do you want to come here to draw or write, Alice?"

"No, thank you."

This thoughtfulness is terrible. Before, *if I happened*

to be at the bureau and he wanted it, he didn't hesitate; he'd say, "Shift your carcass, my dear child, and look smart about it!" Now it's raining again. If we were in Paris . . .

A door slammed and Maria's voice could be heard issuing orders in the distance. Sabot-clad feet ran heavily through the rain. After they had gone past, Alice listened eagerly: "That's all now. They're going to bed." The ashes in the fireplace collapsed and she jumped.

"How nervous you are," said Michel gently. She did not reply but rubbed her shoulderblades against the back of her chair to get rid of the feeling of gooseflesh located in one particular place, the illusion that drops of tepid water were trickling down her back as her husband looked at her.

He's watching me. I know perfectly well I can't stand eleven—no, twelve evenings like this. Nor twelve, no, eleven nights like the one in store for me. What sort of night is in store for me? Oh, I can't stand these drops of tepid water a moment longer.

She turned sharply, recovering her self-possession. *I'm all right; it's only my back that looks frightened.*

"Cigarette, Michel, please?"

He brought the box and the lighter over to her. Between their faces the flame lit up Alice's full, rounded eyelids, her wide mouth closed over the cigarette, her whole face swollen like the mask on a fountain which pours out water. Through her eyelashes she assessed the subtle damage to Michel's features, a kind of shrinkage which seemed to reduce the extent of the cheek and restrict the fine eyes with their sallow rings.

Not good, she decided quickly.

"What are you thinking, Michel? It breaks my heart to look at you. There—and there—"

With one finger she touched first his clean-shaven cheek between the narrow beard and the nose, then the lower eyelid. He shrugged his shoulders.

"I'm thinking that you've been unfaithful to me," he said simply. "What else could I be thinking?"

At first she didn't seem to hear him. She looked at him abstractedly, and from so near at hand that in the irises of her magnificent large eyes he could see slate-blue specks and gray-green streaks converging on a dark center.

"But when," she said finally, "do you think you'll be able to stop thinking about it?"

"I don't know."

"But, Michel, we can't live like this." She turned her head languidly toward the rain-lashed windows.

"It's very kind of you to appreciate the fact."

She swung round on him angrily.

"Neither of us can live like this, Michel! I can't, any more than you! I hate misery, Michel! Being hard up, wearing ourselves out waiting for money to come in, changing jobs, inventing a job, we know what that's like. And in any case, I've been used to that ever since I was a child. But to wallow in emotional misery, to exaggerate everything and advertise it: 'Leave me alone, don't disturb me, I'm miserable.' No, no, for heaven's sake. All this fuss about nothing; it's such an old story. There's nothing to it."

She raised her voice freely, and it was a voice which easily sounded plaintive. At the same time she shook her head in violent, regular movements, as all prisoners do.

"My dear," said Michel, "be patient for a moment. That old story, as far as I'm concerned, only dates back twenty-four hours."

All at once she was silent, assuming the fixed gaze of a somnambulist; her lower lip was relaxed, revealing the brilliant white of her teeth.

He took advantage of her stillness. "Why did you keep the letter?"

"I—I hadn't kept it, I—forgot it," she said weakly, "in the blotter."

"You forgot it, here? Here?" he cried, choking.

"Oh no, not here. The purple blotter belongs to my traveling case."

He sighed with relief. "Oh, well."

"Does that make it easier?" she asked. Her voice was treacherous.

Hurt, he made no reply, but gazed distantly into the fire.

"And if," he ventured after a long silence, "and if there'd been anything else between you and that fellow, anything else rather than what you told me, if—"

"Yes," Alice cut in. "As the man who'd been run over by a bus said, once he got to heaven, 'Now if it had been a Rolls-Royce . . .' "

"My dear, I'm not dead!"

"Thank goodness," she said brutally. "I couldn't forgive you that."

She sat down, crossed her legs, and bent down to put on one of her moccasins. As she leaned forward, long arm dangling against her long thigh, breasts crushed against her knees, her tall figure seemed taller than ever. Michel used to tell her in bed that she was "infinite." "You're as long as a river," he would say, laughing to conceal his crazy, ever-faithful admiration.

While she pushed her foot into the lined slipper with her hand, he secretly observed the freedom of Alice's movements, the suppleness of her knees, her superb back with its long straight furrow, her breasts which were not full—"rather like jellyfish," she would say laughingly—but light. *Won't she ever grow old, then?* he thought angrily. He felt no desire for her and was proud of the fact. *She even revolts me slightly; it's quite natural. Actually giving affectionate friendship and advice to that—fellow, loving interest too, when she was convalescent and weak. She even dared to talk about trust! And if that wasn't enough, she added her entire body, the remains of her high temperature, her wide, slightly rough mouth and her scent. She's . . . they're always worse than we imagine.*

"Tell me," he cried in spite of himself, "did you say *tu* to him?"

She stopped rubbing her bare heel, but didn't understand for a moment, half-closing her eyes as she thought about his question.

"Did I say *tu* to him? Oh no . . . well, sometimes, perhaps."

"Sometimes!" he repeated. "I appreciate the limitation. It—it makes things very clear. It really does."

The face with half-closed eyes became insolent again.

"You asked for that! Perhaps it'll teach you not to ask me any more questions."

He remained motionless, like a man who's injured himself in the dark and daren't take another step.

"Do you know where all this is taking us?" he asked in a low voice.

She sat down in front of the last embers and locked her arms around her knees.

"I've no idea," she said casually.

"It's taking us to the state where many marriages come to grief, a state—I'm speaking for myself—of lukewarm feelings, and semi-indifference. Kindly note that I see the future quite calmly; thank goodness I'm no overenergetic he-man."

"Oh, come out with it," she interrupted contemptuously.

The crash of broken pottery brought her to her feet; Michel had picked up the empty wine jug and thrown it against the wall. He made no other violent gesture and mechanically bent down to pick up the biggest of the fragments, to which an S-shaped handle was still attached, unbroken.

Alice was relieved that Michel had justified and dispelled the fear she had felt trickling down her spine like a drop of lukewarm water, so relieved that she almost condoned his gesture.

"That was stupid," she said, without anger.

"I admit it," said Michel, "but what do you expect?"

He looked carefully at the fragment of pottery hanging by its handle from his slender little finger.

"It's odd; the jug's in pieces and the handle hasn't suffered. Yes, it was stupid. But why does it relieve feelings to do something so silly? Look, the handle had even been mended, and it didn't come off when it fell. That's strange."

"That's strange," repeated Alice.

She pushed the pieces of pottery away with her foot.

"Fortunately the jug was empty," she said casually.

But she had already moved away into the deep recesses of her thoughts and assessed the incident coolly.

We know it relieves our feelings; we know that. So does a blow on the head with a hammer. And two hands clasped rather too tightly around someone's neck. I know someone who'll quietly go and sleep on the divan in the library tonight.

But she didn't. For Michel fell promptly into a light sleep, began to talk in his dreams, and mentioned Alice's name in a loud, confused voice. She stretched out her arm, touched a warm hand that was hanging down from the other bed, and switched on the lamp again. Michel woke up and fell silent, gazing at his wife. From the depths of his dreaming he had recovered happy astonishment and a slightly delirious gratitude. She offered him a glass of water, got up to fold back the old interior shutters and opened the window slightly. A bank of damp air, laden with the green scents that the night and the rain had brought down to ground level, drifted as far as the twin beds, and Michel sat up. But Alice said "Sh, sh," folded the loose arm back on the bed and covered up her husband's shoulder. He obeyed, made himself light, easy and ageless, while she struggled against the need to hear him, to lean over him, over his familiar warm smell, to support him between her shoulder and her ear, in the refuge where a woman nurses the weightiest and dearest burden of her love.

She listened to the battering wind and the fresh gusts of rain. "Sh, sh," she repeated, and the last hours of the spring night passed gently away.

"Such a beautiful jug. If it isn't a shame!"

"It wasn't really beautiful, Maria."

"All the same. . . . Has Madame seen this? The wallpaper's gaping, there. That's new."

"It may be new, but the wallpaper isn't. It must be gaping from boredom."

Alice, wearing gloves, with a scarf tied over her hair, was polishing a brass candlestick, while Maria was moving the bureau, the chairs and the upholstered divan.

"That's exactly what Michel would have said. I'm being nice, too."

Maria, dressed all in black, apart from her close-fitting white cap, was exercising her alertness and powerful, insectlike qualities in an attempt to interpret the secrets of the broken jug. An invisible sun was drying up the nighttime rain in the warm earth, and the soaking-wet garden exhaled a crude smell of flattened grass, *mousserons* and sprouting tubers.

"What does Madame think is wrong with Monsieur?"

Unhurriedly Alice shook out her yellow duster over the laurustinus.

"He's been overworking. He was out of sorts when he came from Paris—a touch of flu."

Maria approved of these three suggestions, nodding her broad grasshopper's forehead.

She's talking today, thought Alice. *She's flitting around this broken jug like a dragonfly over a pond. And he's asleep next door with a temperature of 38.3°.*

"Is Madame going to send for the doctor?"

Alice finished dusting the bars of a chair, stood up straight and faced Maria. "No. If his temperature goes up tonight I'll telephone Dr. Puymaigre tomorrow morning. But—" She appeared to be examining the remains of the jug which Maria had collected in the wastepaper basket. "But I don't think it will. It's nerves, really."

Maria picked up the wastepaper basket with her small strong hand and shook the fragments of pottery as though she were jingling coins in a church collection. "Was it Madame who dropped the jug?"

"No," said Alice sharply. "It was Monsieur. It doesn't matter who did it—it comes to the same thing in the end."

The servant's eyes moved thoughtfully from the torn wallpaper down to the floor, estimating the distance between the bureau and the exact spot where the jug had fallen.

"Oh, it was Monsieur," she stated. "Well, he shouldn't have."

For the second time, Alice detected somewhere beneath Maria's unyielding exterior a sign of human warmth, an instinct she compared to the solidarity linking wife and concubine. A flush suffused her whole face, even to her eyelids, swollen after a sleepless night.

A fine conquest. A treacherous peasant woman, devoured with curiosity, who's never relished my presence here. But she hasn't accepted my presence. I can't call her treacherous—I've seen no underhand behavior. How penetrating she is! In fact, what can I reproach her for? Ferocious honesty? All her virtues?

She leaned against the window, forgetting her housework, looking out over the tangled greenery and its glitter of rain, decked out with short-lived flowers, barely opened leaves, and buds still red from their painful efforts toward maturing.

How lovely it was, two days ago . . .

A barely perceptible path led down to the darkest place in the wood, toward the wild strawberries in flower, the tall gaunt stalks of Solomon's-seal and new, uncurling fronds of bracken.

I shan't be going out exploring in that wood by myself today. And will I be going with Michel? No.

She reassured herself by listening to Maria, who was polishing the floor with felt pattens on her feet, her lean brown arms swinging out loosely in a regular rhythm, her goat legs dancing with scissorlike movements. She moved over the polished oak floor like a water spider over the pewter surface of a pond. Alice lingered, feeling a humble pleasure at the sound of the felt-clad feet. She would have enjoyed, too, the sound of the pestle and mortar, the broom in the vestibule, the ax on the chopping block, all the signs of Maria's presence.

I'd like, she sighed inwardly, *to sort lentils in the kitchen, or pull out grass from the paths. I'd like to go to the fair at Sarzat-le-Haut. But I'm not overjoyed at the idea of giving lemonade and fruit salts to that man in there with his temperature 38.3°. I'm quite happy to look after him, but not when he's ill.* As she went through the library, she ventured a piece of advice to Maria.

"You know, Maria, it's very bad for your insides to polish the floor like that, with your feet."

She didn't wait for an answer and felt slightly ashamed of herself as she went out. *Advances—I'm almost making advances to her now.* Behind her the dancing pattens stopped for a moment, then began again with a kind of furious gaiety.

She went into the half-darkness of the bedroom, glass tinkling on the small tray she was carrying.

"Aren't you asleep? Are you better? Here's the hot lemonade. Show me your tongue. More. . . . It looks awful! What about your bowels? When did you last . . ."

He squirmed under the bedclothes. "Leave me alone! I hate this kind of inquisition!"

"Come on, Michel, you must. Don't be childish!"

He hunched himself up and pushed the tray away with a hostile, childish expression.

"Michel! I will *not* allow you to neglect yourself. Drink it up quickly. I've put a large spoonful of salts in it. You must stay in bed until—until you have to run.

And you won't get up until teatime, at five o'clock."

Patiently she watched him drink. But she was glad to get away, and moved too rapidly.

"Where are you going now?"

She stopped as though her bridle had been jerked.

"Now? I'm going—just outside. Just into the garden. Nowhere, actually." She looked down. "Nowhere," she repeated.

Before she closed the door she had an idea. "Oh, Michel. If there's a telephone call from Paris—"

"Well, I'm here," he said, in the voice of an able-bodied man.

"If you're asleep, shall I take it?"

He turned his head on the pillow, looked Alice up and down as she stood there in her morning clothes, ringed with silver light coming in from the garden, and bestowed on her a somewhat unpleasant smile.

"No, you mustn't. That's exactly what you mustn't do. Just call out to me, that's all."

She didn't reply and went out, congratulating herself on her moderation, then transformed her solitude into a legitimate reward, going thoughtfully and quietly from the terrace to the garden, from the garden to the house. The sun looked white, continually muffled by lazy clouds that threatened storms but never produced them and imposed a truce of silence on the nightingales. At noon Maria served luncheon on the terrace: cabbage stuffed with minced meat and rice, the leaves baked to a golden brown.

"Leftovers, I admit," the servant said coldly, making

her excuses. "Since nobody went down to the shops this morning."

"If I had leftovers like this in Paris, Maria . . ."

She ate hungrily and quickly; the soft, sad light fell on her smooth hair, which mirrored the fleecy sky, and her pale, heavy-lidded eyes. At the same time she listened to what was going on in the house, heard Michel's quick step, the banging of secret doors and the fastening of a certain bolt. *So everything's all right. His temperature won't go up again tonight.*

"What else are you bringing me, Maria?"

"My melon preserve. Taste it, Madame. I always put four lemons in it to give a bit of taste."

The two women, one seated and the other standing, were both thinking that they were alone together for the first time, and they felt strangely moved.

How odd. The first time. Between us there's always been Michel, or Maria's husband, or a washerwoman, a ladder for cleaning the windows, a preserve pan.

"Four lemons. So that's the secret! Well, I would never have guessed! I was just saying to myself—"

The telephone bell silenced her, altered the benevolent gray of the sky and the pink hawthorn. Alice put her spoon down on her plate.

"Oh, that bell. We ought to change it."

"Will Madame be answering it?"

She replied with a negative sign, already waiting for the sound of her husband's voice, the way he said "Hullo, yes, hullo!"—the uncompromising way he treated subordinates when he wasn't looking at them.

As soon as contact was made he lowered his voice, and Alice could hear only a friendly murmur.

"I'll take my coffee out here, Maria. Pour it out yourself and just bring me a full cup. Two lumps of sugar, as usual."

She began to listen again, craning her neck and concentrating until she was dazed. She thought she heard a complaisant half-laugh and screwed up her lips malevolently. But after a long silence she heard him call out in near-desperation, "Don't cut me off!" Then Michel's voice rose, expressing astonishment, and was interrupted by the caller. "There can't be any discussion about that sort of thing!" he shouted. "No! I won't allow it! There's only one way of looking at the terms. What do you mean, I'm supposed to have trusted . . ."

That's it, said Alice to herself. *And a good thing too.* She went on listening, in vain. Her cigarette, which was shaking as she held it, touched the remains of the preserve on her plate and went out. She didn't know that she was going pale, but Maria, who was bringing the cup of steaming coffee, looked at her and paused. At the same moment Michel appeared on the threshold, slamming the door loudly behind him, and Alice, instinctively getting up to run away from him, stumbled. She encountered beside her Maria's outstretched arm, her shoulder as hard as a board, all her lean, gnarled strength.

"Now then, Madame, now then," said the servant under her breath.

"Did you hear?" shouted Michel from a distance.

She shook her head and sat down again. As Michel walked rapidly toward her, she bit her chapped white lip.

"Maria, have you any coffee left? Would you bring me a drop, please?"

He sat down on the bench by his wife. Seeing him bright-eyed and in good spirits, she relaxed and took a deep breath in order to subdue the beating of her heart.

"Now," said Michel. "Do you think that in . . . four or five days you could produce sketches for most of the costumes for *Daffodyl,* thinking of a smaller cast, of course. It's always the shows you think dead and buried that come to life again. Didn't you think it was all up with that one? I didn't think it was worth a damn. Only, now that they want the theatre, I wouldn't dream of their using the old costumes from the original production; they're all stained with cleaning fluid; they're worn out after two hundred performances. They'll take your costumes! I've told them so! At least you must sell your designs and make a profit! A promise is a promise! I told them straight—"

"Them? Who is that?" asked Alice.

Michel's animation subsided. He took a full coffee cup from Maria's hands and waited until she had left.

"It's still the Bordat and Hirsch group," he said. "I don't think the bid will come off; you must realize that. I think they're reviving *Daffodyl* a year too soon. But I've got the theatre! While they were still writing letters I didn't take it seriously. These people only mean business when they get someone to telephone."

"Who telephoned?" asked Alice.

He sipped his coffee, pretended he had burned his lips, took his time, and looked hard at his wife. Since he could no longer avoid answering her, he made it sound offensive.

"Ambrogio, naturally. Who else would they get to telephone except Ambrogio? He's my partner—if I dare use that expression."

He stood up, walked a few steps and then came back. "Well? Is that all you've got to say?"

She bestowed upon him her most sleepy-looking gaze. "What? What do I say? Oh yes—well, I say yes."

"What does 'yes' mean?"

"I'll produce the designs."

"In four days' time?"

"I've already got forty-four sketches. As for the ballet costumes—"

Michel laughed briefly, sounding ironic and commercial-minded.

"I don't think you need worry too much about the ballet costumes, for a very good reason."

"What's that?"

"Well. . . . Four little classical dancers who'll dance on points."

"Tarlatan," said Alice quickly.

"Yes. Two good acrobatic dancers."

"Nude effect, slashing, and strass."

"Strass?" objected Michel. "Do you think you're in 1913? No extravagance. Sequins would be all right. That won't let them in for much. They can't be let in for much anyway. Not over the soloists either. They'll beat you down, you know."

Alice seemed to wake up and became cheerful.

"The soloists? Flowers by the yard instead of feathers, ribbons instead of embroidery, cellophane to give a silky look, and fringing for luxury effects. Yes, I understand!"

"Have you got the sketches here?"

"Yes, all of them. In my purple blotter," she added thoughtlessly.

How to put your foot in it, she thought as she watched Michel drain his coffee cup. His mouth looked bitter. *I'll have to remove from my vocabulary the words "blotter" and "purple," or else, every time I use them, I'll have to see the leaves drooping on this sensitive plant. But the same sensitive plant has friendly talks on the telephone with Ambrogio. Strange, even bizarre, as my late father used to say.*

Her hands were getting cold. She rubbed them together and shivered as though from some kind of shame. *It's terrible to realize all that's changed between us. The slightest remark makes him shrink. He looks withered and old; his right eye's growing smaller. And I never miss an opportunity to criticize him, as though it were his fault that I went to bed with Ambrogio.*

"Michel, I'm just going to put on a dress and go down to the village."

"To the village?"

"I've got no sketching materials. No paper, no colors, no tracing paper."

"Do you want to do some drawings?" he asked absentmindedly.

"Think, Michel, my costumes!"

"Of course; I'm sorry."

"Is there anything you want?"

The look he gave his wife revealed his devotion to his own suffering.

"Yes, there is. But the thing I want is something you can't give me."

He blushed like a young man and walked back into the house with long strides.

Behind him she bit her lip, called him a sentimental fool, threw her napkin down in a rage and tossed her head back in order to catch two tears between her eyelashes. Half an hour later she was walking down the hill, holding up her face to the drops of rain that fell now and then. On the way she planned costumes, calculated cost prices and picked the first self-heal flowers. *I'll use this little horn-tipped crest for the fairy's headdress in* Daffodyl.

In the village she bought schoolchildren's crayons, bottles of red and purple ink and watercolor paints destined for young beginners.

"They can be chewed without any danger," the shopkeeper assured her.

She went back up the hill feeling more cheerful and full of goodwill. On the way she sat down to draw the Snail's costume on her new sketchpad. The rain, which was as fine as sea mist, clung to her powdered cheeks and her hair. "An hour on your own and a little work

—all you need for a good complexion and a good temper too!"

When she reached the terrace, a strip of golden sky on the horizon was the only area to escape the invading rain clouds.

"Michel, where are you?" she called.

It was Maria who appeared at the door, her hands gloved in flour. "Has Monsieur gone out, Maria?"

"Monsieur is in the library. Monsieur hasn't stirred."

"Did you take him a warm drink, Maria?"

"Yes, but Monsieur snubbed me; he didn't drink it."

Maria's eloquent eyes looked down, and she shook her black-clad arms with their white mittens.

"Monsieur was on the telephone. I may have disturbed him."

She raised her face to Alice, her new "distant ally" face, and then, awkwardly, fled.

"Another telephone call. . . . And he hasn't been out. And he didn't drink the—"

She hesitated and then went into the house with a great deal of noise, having decided to act casually.

"Are you there? My goodness, how dark it is in here! You can't imagine the sort of artist's materials they have here! And you can't get tracing paper! But that's Cransac. When it comes to survival, I've known worse. I've brought the papers. Has anything happened?"

"Not much. I've got a ghastly migraine! Oh, there was a telephone call."

"Who was it?"

"Those people, you know, the Hirsch and Bordat

people. Terribly sorry, my dear, but it's all off."

"What is?"

"The *Daffodyl* business."

"What do you mean?"

"Yes. *Daffodyl's* not going on at L'Etoile after all."

He moved again, as though embarrassed, and turned over on the divan.

"Oh . . . oh no," faltered Alice. "That's a bit much."

She sat down, untied her little parcels mechanically and lit the lamp on the bureau.

"Now tell me about it."

"I tell you, I've got a terrible headache," groaned Michel.

"You must take some aspirin. But first tell me what happened."

He replied with bad grace, turning to the wall. "What is there to tell? When something falls through, that's it."

"Is it a question of cash?"

"Yes, that too . . . complications . . . Hirsch can't lend his name to the thing, neither as a sleeping partner nor as a director."

"But what about you?"

"They don't want me on my own. I'm not really their man."

Alice looked hard at the curly head and the body which seemed to be talking into the wall.

"Couldn't you and Ambrogio act together?"

Michel didn't reply.

"Did you hear what I said? You and Ambrogio? He

belongs to their camp, doesn't he?"

She watched Michel's back as his breathing became jerky.

"You make me laugh," he said condescendingly.

She thought for a moment, chewing the stalk of the self-heal flower that was now useless.

"It was you who called Paris," she said.

He moved, turning one side of his face toward her. "Why do you ask me that?"

"I'm not asking you. I'm telling you: it was you who called Paris."

He replied only with a shrug of his shoulders and turned back toward the wall.

"You've played a dirty trick," said Alice after a moment. "You've wrecked the whole thing."

He sat up and smoothed down his hair with the flat of his hand.

"Yes," he repeated. "I've wrecked the whole thing. Must I tell you why?"

"No," she said, her thoughts far away. "No. I can see it clearly enough. In fact, you could only have been a kind of minor director *vis-à-vis* Ambrogio, who's on very good terms with the Hirsch people. My work with him over the costumes and scenery . . . I see. You decided to wreck the whole thing, didn't you? Isn't that the situation, more or less?"

"More or less."

Michel was swaying backward and forward, his hands between his knees.

"Was it Ambrogio who took your call?"

"Yes, of course."

"And . . . what does he think about your refusal?"

Michel began to laugh, without looking at his wife.

"Ambrogio? He believes I'm right, really, you know. He thinks it's a dirty trick and that Hirsch and Bordat will come back to us at the first opportunity with a better offer. Nobody could be more optimistic, as you can see."

"Indeed."

He stopped swaying and questioned Alice with a barely concealed effort. "And what about you? What have you got to say about my refusal?"

She restrained conflicting feelings and tried to analyze them.

"I? I think you're throwing away a nice amount of money, but that's your problem. You don't usually pay much attention to my opinion, at least in business matters."

"Don't play with words, Alice. I'm really not myself today. Try to look at things another way. A woman who can inspire such jealousy, jealousy that's more important than money, commonsense and everything—some women—in my opinion, my humble opinion—would be proud of it."

"Michel, don't ever do anything so dangerous as deciding what makes a woman feel proud or not."

"Oh, I know."

She leaned forward. Her bold mouth, her nose with its flattened nostrils, emerged from the area of darkness.

"No, you don't know. Neither do I. I can't understand what you think about me since . . . But I'm beginning to think that a man and a woman can do everything together without any trouble, except make conversation. Whenever one of us says something now, ever since that day, the other listens politely as if he were deaf, or else replies from a hundred miles away, from heaven knows where, from a reef where he makes signals, lost and solitary. No, I beg of you! We'll drive each other mad again. *Daffodyl* is dead. Let's bury *Daffodyl.*"

She revived the somnolent fire, patted her damp fringe against her forehead, sat in her favorite chair, took a blue crayon and began to draw a pointed flowery cap for some little stage fairy. Behind her, in the shadow, she heard a deep, jerky sigh of gratitude. She took the trouble to seem preoccupied with her drawing and examined it at arm's length, her head on one side, screwing up her eyes. She listened to the fine rain, the crackling fire, the little owl-faced clock perched high up near the ceiling, and thought: *It's only six o'clock. It's only Saturday. Ten whole days still to come. . . .* She gave up the Fairy's costume for the Dragonfly's. *Cellophane wings, the whole body in articulated plaques of light metal, with just a coat of Duco; I can see wonderful blues and greens. The eyes, yes, the eyes. . . . Two little balloons of iridescent rubber, on each side of the head. Pretty. But that's more for revue than musical comedy.* Mesmerized by the music of the raindrops falling on to the balcony under the broken gutter, she allowed her crayon to stray over the paper.

"And on top of that," came Michel's voice, "they wanted us to leave for Paris tonight, or tomorrow morning at the latest."

She didn't reply, tore up her sketch, and on a piece of blank paper began to draw door handles and radiator screens.

"Just now," the voice went on, "the thought of seeing those people again . . . just now . . . well, I'm not proud of myself, and it doesn't say much for my character, but I must admit . . ."

. . . *that it would be too much for me,* concluded Alice to herself. *When Michel starts a sentence, he could always hand it over for someone else to finish. Clause in parentheses and cliché, cliché and clause in parentheses. Poor Michel, how badly I treat him. How would I treat him if I didn't love him? My drawing's hideous. Early metro style exactly. I'd never dare offer these horrible things to the Eschenbach studies."*

She rolled the sheet of paper into a ball and with the colored crayons tried out a design for a necklace, belt and bracelet which at first satisfied her. *Plaques of thick glass. Metal balls here, and hardwood. Or lacquered prune pits. Result: ugly, shoddy stuff, Uganda style. Oh, I'm off form.* She pushed the crayons and drawing paper away and listened to the raindrops falling musically into a pool of water. *They're singing, "E,G, G,E,G,G sharp."*

"And if," the voice went on uncertainly, "and if I had the consolation—no, what am I saying? After all, yes, it is a consolation—if I could tell myself that only a sudden sexual impulse . . ."

Alice clenched her teeth. "It's starting all over again."

"For a woman, a well-balanced woman, that is, a violent sexual urge is almost always an abnormal crisis, some morbid incident. Do you understand what I'm saying, Alice?"

"Very well." *And I'm keeping serious, what's more,* she said to herself. *It's true that I don't giggle easily these days. But why can't men ever talk about a woman's sensuality without saying something utterly stupid?*

Heartened, Michel got up, then walked with long measured steps, stretching out his arms to show that he was going forward to meet equity and encounter meekness. But when he reached the end of the room, between the two bookcases, he turned on his heel with a violence that constantly belied his laborious display of good-natured behavior.

"A passing fancy, of course, a passing fancy . . . I admit. And even if. . . . What can I do? I'm made that way."

She continued to draw in casual fashion, either looking at him furtively or listening carefully. She heard a few words here and there, variations on a persistent theme. When Michel stopped by the table and used the lighter to light his cigarette, Alice was suddenly aroused and absorbed by the deterioration of his features. *What havoc in such a short time! He looks as though he's been made up. He's deadly boring, but he's wasting away. He hardly eats a thing, he plays with his food. I'll put up with anything, but not the sight of him wasting away. His face is getting thinner, his left eye's smaller, and that nasty little laugh. . . . My poor Michel! Just the way he looked when the Spéleïeff collapse put us in a spot, and finally he got paratyphoid.*

She knitted her brows, borne up by a kind of affectionate malice that was still lacking in direction but intervened in advance between Michel and illness, Michel and danger, Michel and the injuries which Alice inflicted on him. She followed him with her eyes as he walked up and down like a maniac, and then looked away because she had gazed at him ardently.

"And you'll admit that I'm not completely in the wrong? Alice? I say, Alice!"

"Sorry."

"My goodness, she's not even listening to me!" He placed his hand over her head with indignant tenderness. "My poor little wretch," he said.

She excused herself with a restrained smile. "You mustn't be cross with me, Michel. I'm trying to pick up the pieces. Are you going to break something every day? Leave us in peace for a moment, or at least let's have a little silence." She pushed the lamp toward him. "Here, let's share the papers. I'll take the picture pages . . ."

He's turning me into a coward, she thought. *The terrible thing is that I'm getting used to the situation. If he'd treated me as a poor little wretch two days ago, there would have been hell to pay. How many hours have gone by without our insulting each other? If I were to let him do as he liked, he'd get used to it. Being miserable every day, saying "if only" every day, every day's like an extra year. And on high days and holidays, embraces filled with shame, more remorse, erotico-infernal mentions of the famous Ambrogio . . . Ambrogio! He's thinking about Ambrogio. . . .*

Coldly, she recomposed the features of the subtle man from Nice whose black hair shone like a bird's plumage. *The color of his lips was attractive, barely red, rather a pinkish beige. . . . He had beautiful gums that framed the top of his teeth like tiny pink arcades . . . and plenty of other merits. . . .* She used the past tense, as though speaking of someone who was dead: Thinking about Ambrogio . . . *Do I ever think about him?*

Silently she lowered the illustrated magazine she was leafing through. The way Michel's newspaper jerked in his hands echoed the irregular, rapid beating of an exhausted heart.

He's thinking about him. I'll wait two or three days more . . . and then I'll risk it.

She waited. But she was clumsy enough to let him see that she was waiting. The waiting, the way her blood throbbed slightly in her ears, the daily sound of the telephone ringing, the bell on the postman's bicycle, the invisible trains which crossed the river and left a horizontal white cloud over the valley—everything she heard, everything she saw reminded Alice that she was thinking about time; she began to crane her neck forward and to look slightly bemused.

"What are you listening to?" Michel would ask.

Calmly she would tell him a lie. "A mouse in the rafters. I thought the shutter outside the kitchen window was banging."

One evening he caught her pretending to read, her eyes fixed vacantly on the area of darkness that lay between the two bookcases.

"What's so interesting over there?"

"Nothing. The dark," she replied.

He smiled. "Oh, so you look at the dark too, do you?"

"Yes, I do. What a lovely time we're having," she said gloomily. As she turned toward him, her neck still looked smooth and flexible. "Michel, why don't we go back to Paris tomorrow?"

He frowned deeply and went on the defensive: "Back to Paris? Are you out of your mind? When we've still got nine days' holiday before taking over from Ambrogio? When I'm trying to recover my balance and—"

"Don't shout," Alice interrupted. "The windows are open."

"You go back to Paris, then! I'm not forcing anyone to spend a boring time here; I don't expect anyone to be helpful, understanding, or—"

"Oh, very well, let's pretend I said nothing. I'm not unhappy here myself."

He put down his spectacles and looked carefully at his wife's face.

"That's not true," he said harshly. "You *are* unhappy here. But I don't see why you should be happy. Why should you be happy when you don't deserve to be?"

"Because I want to be."

"That's a fine reason!"

"It's the best one. You're talking to me about what I deserve! What has deserving got to do with the need to take deep breaths, have a good complexion and not punish yourself every morning?"

"You should only talk about things you know," said Michel. "Punishing yourself! Mortification and you—"

"You'd better say 'mortification and us'! When you're talking business you sometimes bite the inside of your cheek to stop yourself from hitting someone. I know how to manage without anything that isn't essential; in other words, I don't buy clothes and I don't take any rest, in order to have some things that are necessities. As far as asceticism goes, there's nothing to choose between us."

"Necessities? What necessities?"

She shrugged her shoulders in her own individual way, as though she wanted to shake off her dress and walk away naked.

"Love, for instance; our love. A car when I want one. The right to send certain people to hell. An old tailored suit but a good petticoat underneath. I drink water all year round, but I need a freezer to make it cool. A lot of little things. They're necessities, I think."

She went out, for she didn't want to see him look upset, and swore firmly to herself: *Tomorrow, and not a day later!*

The next night she slept badly. She always became anxious early in the night, feeling faint-hearted and shaky, and only found her confidence again between midnight and dawn. Her forehead and her knees touched the wall, and she lay as far away as she could from the adjoining bed where Michel, who had taken a double dose of aspirin, was lying utterly still, breathing quietly.

It was I who advised him to double the dose, thought

Alice. *One gram is a lot. When he's taken one gram I can't hear him breathing. These beds standing so close to each other, side by side—what a barbarous idea! A double bed is all right, but these twin beds, these observation posts. During the summer holidays I'll change this unsatisfactory bedroom. But what sort of summer holidays will we have?*

Scattered elements of a dream mingled together: the squat towers of Cransac, the tall dark figure of Chevestre—*like a priest, like a priest,* she would hum to herself—endless sheets of multicolored paper flying through the air, the whole thing dissolving into the impenetrable darkness that brooded between the two tall, impassive bookcases. She thought in her dream that she was getting up, collecting the papers together and running away. But all at once the sound of the first blackbird subdued the dazzling monotony of the nightingales, forced its way across the threshold of the dream and spoke to Alice of dawn. She relaxed her knees, loosened her tense arms and, now reassured, glided into sleep.

The next morning her anxiety awoke before she did, and the last moments of her dream repeated one phrase over and over again: "I'll go tomorrow, I'll go tomorrow . . ."

No, today, she corrected herself as she opened her eyes. Michel was sleeping as though remote from his body, his face pale and calm. She didn't wake him but looked at him with commiseration. *He's young, when he's asleep. I'll go today. With so much ahead of us, we need something really cheering to eat.* She put on her moccasins and the white flannel wrapper and went off to find Maria, who was emptying the ashes from the stove and keeping an eye on the milk and coffee which were steaming on the red-hot embers of the stove, inlaid with old blue tiles.

"Maria, I'm determined that Monsieur should get his appetite back."

"So am I," said Maria.

Her glance took in Alice's pallor, and wrinkles appeared on her broad forehead.

"If cooking has anything to do with it," she concluded. "Would Madame move out of the way, please? My milk's going to boil over."

She placed a spoon in the milk, which was rising, and moved the saucepan from the heat. She wore her white cap and was dressed in her eternal black. *Does she ever take her clothes off?* wondered Alice.

"What's happened to your arm, Maria? Is it a burn? Or a cut?"

"It's practically nothing," said Maria.

"Practically nothing under a bandage that's very badly tied?"

"Is it a good thing to put butter on a burn?"

"It doesn't do any harm. But there are better things. And better bandages, too."

"It's not bad, considering I did it with one hand. Look, Madame: put on with one hand and fastened up with my teeth."

"Couldn't your husband help you?"

Maria's eyes shone and laughed among her wrinkles. "He helped me, all right. But not with the bandaging."

They stood there together, both of the same height, and talked quietly. Alice broke off the corners from the pieces of toasted bread and munched them. The bitter aroma of coffee brought moisture into her dry mouth and she allowed herself a comforting pause. *How clean it all is; it's all so well organized; how feminine it all is here.* Suddenly she saw in front of her a vivid picture of the Vaugirard studio, its superficial untidiness and its complicated cleanliness.

"Undo that, Maria. I'm going to make a wonderful bandage for you."

"In my kitchen!" said Maria, shocked.

"In your kitchen, precisely."

Out of modesty the servant placed a saucepan lid over the milk. Then with her free hand she unwound the bandage with ceremonial slowness and held out her forearm to Alice as though she were giving her the keys of a conquered city.

"Oh!" said Alice. "Was it boiling water or the edge of the stove?"

"No, Madame. The poker."

"The poker? How could it be the poker?"

They looked at each other, and Maria began to laugh.

"It's a guessing game. Can't Madame guess who gave me this?"

With her chin she indicated the open window and,

beyond, the orchard and the vegetable plots.

"It was that one there—the halfwit. The man with the big backside. That soft thing."

"Your husband? What's got into him?"

"He's having his revenge."

"What for?"

"For the fact that he's my husband and I'm his wife. That's quite enough. Doesn't Madame agree?"

She laughed scornfully and fingered the blister full of water, and the rim of swollen flesh that surrounded it.

"Don't touch your burn!" cried Alice. "I'm going to drain the blister first."

Doesn't Madame agree? she repeated to herself. *Oh yes, oh yes, Madame* does *agree* . . . She concentrated, avoiding any reply, and the knowing Maria was satisfied by her silence.

"So Madame and Monsieur want to eat well tonight? It's late to tell me that. We'll have to eat game from the farmyard. Suppose I did pigeons disguised as partridges? Or should Escudière kill six birds for me? Or should I do the duck? But eating duck makes you dream."

While she talked, Alice was bandaging a thin, flat forearm with slender bones. Beneath the crumpled skin, the old scars and the amber-colored calluses she could read the story of a hand which had once been beautiful. She touched long fingers, a palm as rough and warm as an espalier wall.

"I'm not hurting you, am I?"

Maria replied only with a sign, and her thanks were brief:

"That was a good piece of work, Madame. Well done, it was." But before unrolling her sleeve, she bent her head and laid the white bandage close against her cheek, as she might have hugged a newborn baby in its swaddling clothes.

"I've got three cards," announced Alice.

"They're no good," said Michel.

They were trying to play piquet. A cigarette between her lips, Alice was tilting her head to one side and screwing up her eyes to avoid the rising smoke.

"Put your cigarette down," advised Michel.

"Why?"

"It doesn't look nice. And it's not chic to smoke like that."

"I can't smoke or play any other way. I've also got a tierce."

She coughed.

"There, you see! That cigarette-end's making your eyes smart and it makes you cough too. It's rather odd; I find that when women take up a man's habit, they take up all its messiness and often all its ugliness. That's just what you do."

"Yes, Mama," said Alice. "I have a tierce, as I said, and I'd like you to know that it's a major tierce, in clubs. It's your bid."

Michel didn't reply at once, and as she looked up she could see on his face the anger of desire, the need to be violent and possessive. "Heavens! Isn't that going to make things more complicated for me?" When he had counted up the points that she had been writing down on a score pad, she deliberately stuck another cigarette in the corner of her mouth, holding her head at an even more blasé angle. She was glad that their conflict and all its attendant risks were leading him toward dangerous and well-known terrain.

The evening before, she had planned for Michel a carefully cooked dinner, full of enticing flavors, but in vain; he had not condescended to eat it; he merely drank and called out, "Brava, bravi, bravo!" to Maria, who was absentminded and rather cold. *Maria's like an animal with a good sense of smell; she deserts men or other animals when they're hurt or ill. I'll wait another twenty-four hours.*

Since the previous day she had felt time passing slowly and had put things off until tomorrow as much from cowardice as from diplomacy. Since the day before, the district had been lashed with rain; a curtain of rain hung down over Cransac, through which Alice and Michel, who were now cut off, could distinguish the muddy patch of red hawthorn and the flowering currant with their bunches of pink flowers. They watched the rain beating down on the terrace and spurting up again in watery suckerlike sprays. Since the previous day they had had no other distractions apart from books, the fire, the unrelenting rain itself—"like the rain in a film," said Michel. Maria would run out to the woodshed with an apron over her head. When her husband went down to the village he would turn up the little collar on his jacket and open a tattered umbrella. But Alice and Michel soon tired of talk about the rain and the sudden misdeeds of the river which were reported to them in lugubrious terms by Maria.

"Monsieur, the water's coming into the vegetable garden! And the road's flooded! Has Monsieur ever seen anything like it?"

"Yes," said Michel, "about ten times in ten years. But you've got a memory like a newborn babe!"

The day before, Alice, while standing in a state of feverish idleness in front of the window, besought Michel with a look, showing him, outside, the silvery bars of the watery prison.

"Be patient awhile," replied Michel. "We can't drive in such a deluge. As soon as it brightens, we'll think about going back. In fact, I believe that spring has gone to pieces."

Since the day before they hadn't upset each other. *The rain truce,* thought Alice.

She shuffled the cards, dealt them and arranged her hand like a fan, her head on one side and a cigarette between her lips.

"What is the Lautrec painting you remind me of?" asked Michel.

Glancing at him swiftly, she saw that he was looking at her with hostile admiration.

"A Lautrec that's hard to live with, I'm sure. Careful, Michel; do you know I need only twenty-two points? You're absolutely hopeless."

A dull warmth and a feeling of unease akin to desire betrayed her husband's agitation. She could visualize their embrace, a favorite kind of libertinage, the conventional gratitude that would follow it. *And then what? After that, I wouldn't dare—I won't want to carry out my decision anymore. After that he'll regard me as too important. Come on, now. . . .* She allowed her face to lose all expression, put down her cigarette, and added up the score with a look of concentration that Michel called her European look.

"You owe me an incredible amount of money, Michel. Thirty-two francs. You absolutely insisted on losing—"

She remembered the traditional joke about being lucky in love.

"Will you let me have my revenge?"

"No, Michel! I don't want to start losing, and I'm going to have a glass of anisette."

She disliked dry liqueurs and only enjoyed the sweet, syrupy ones flavored with fennel, vanilla and orange. As she held the bottle, it clinked against the glass. *It's ridiculous; my hand's shaking.*

"Whatever's the matter?" asked Michel.

She knew that raised voice which became exceptionally clear when he was angry or suspicious. As she came back toward Michel she swallowed half her glass of liqueur in one gulp, and felt stronger.

He's got such sharp ears. If he didn't know me so well, I could reply, "A touch of malaria," and I'd pretend to be interesting. But he knows I've never had malaria. Nor indigestion. Nor anything else . . . except a slight yearning for my years between fifteen and twenty-five. Oh, that time when we hardly knew each other, when everyone was talking to him about me, they used to say, "But she's the least interesting of the four girls!" How new everything was! He would look me up and down in amazement: "Good heavens!" he'd say, and I'd listen to him and say, "Oh!" It was wonderful. He was keeping up appearances as director of The Gossip, *which didn't earn him anything, but his horrible little dive where people drank lemonade and listened to songs was making a fortune. . . .*

She sighed deeply, in silence. The heavy rain fell steadily and noisily on the tiled attic roofs. The leaking gutter sobbed out its water onto the balcony, and from time to time drops of rain fell down the unprotected chimney into the fireplace, hissing as they touched the ashes and imitating the weeping of the damp woods. Michel, who felt the cold, covered his knees with the tartan rug that was full of moth holes and cigarette burns.

"Are you shivering too? It's because you've got a slight temperature. I'm shivering for another reason, Michel."

There! She congratulated herself. *Like that I'm burning my boats. I have to talk now.* She almost remained silent, however, for Michel immediately looked at her intelligently, with a gaze that asked no questions.

"Michel, I must tell you . . ."

Furtively he placed his hand over the region of his

liver, then moved it to his neck and loosened his silk scarf.

"No, no, Michel. I don't want to hurt you; anything but. Don't be afraid."

She stretched her long hand timidly toward him, but with a slight shrug he moved away, just far enough to be out of her reach.

"Afraid?" he said. "Afraid, am I! I'm not afraid. Who do you think you are, I wonder?"

She regretted having used the worst possible word, the one that male susceptibility cannot tolerate, and then she became clumsier than ever:

"I'm expressing myself badly. I wanted you to understand that—what I'm going to tell you isn't so terribly serious—" She stammered and her chin trembled.

"You seem very upset to me. Do you want to tell me something that's not too serious? If your face is anything to go by, it's not too pleasant either. But take your time, my dear, take your time."

He cocked his ear toward the miniature cascade tumbling down from the gutter and turned his golden, amused eyes toward his wife again. "I don't expect to go out tonight."

She shrugged. "Jokes won't help either of us, especially that sort of joke. Nothing's easy between you and me, Michel."

She sat down, feeling dizzy from the small quantity of anisette she had drunk; with the tips of her fingers she touched a small piece of folded paper in the pocket of her white jacket.

"Michel, I want to tell you the truth."

He remained on the defensive and began to laugh.

"Again! You want to tell me the truth again? In the first place, what truth? I know one truth, and I can assure you it's quite enough for me. I can even say I've had more than enough. Is there another truth to come? My God! *Il pleut des vérités premières,/Tendez vos rouges tabliers*. . . . Is that it? What did you say?"

"Me? Nothing. I'm waiting for you to finish. Is it so hard to be straightforward?"

He lowered his eyes. His tone and his expression changed:

"Yes, my poor child, it's very difficult, I assure you. When you suffer the way I'm suffering, you've got just enough strength not to be straightforward, that is to say, to put a brave face on things, more or less, not to go for—oh, I don't know—drink, jumping in the river, sleeping pills . . ." He sat down heavily close to her. "It's odd, all the same, how dependent one is on the quality of some unhappiness or treachery. I wouldn't have believed it. I've told you already, once, twice, twenty times over: if it had been a case of—"

She jumped up and ran toward him. "Exactly! Oh, Michel, listen, it's all my fault. I should have talked about it earlier. Michel, it's a good thing—"

She sounded too cheerful, and realized it. *After all, it's no fun for him, after all.* She wanted him to be curious by now, anxious. But he avoided her and sat with one shoulder hunched up, narrowing his eyes. She tried out the effect of her delightful, plaintive voice.

"Help me a little, Michel! You can see I'm struggling!"

"Most of all," he said, "I can see that you're like a cold draught. What a lot of preambles and flourishes! What a lot of noise! Truth's a very noisy business!"

She flushed, feeling humiliated in her attempts at peacemaking.

"Very well. Then I'll be quick and waste no words. In fact, you've told me often enough that you'd have preferred"—she corrected herself—"that you would have been less upset if . . ."

He motioned to her, silencing the words she was about to utter.

"Yes, yes, go on."

"And that your indulgence, your understanding at least—"

"Yes, yes—"

"—would have been won over by . . ."

He clenched his fist and pressed it against his teeth: "Oh, for God's sake!"

She burst out, driven beyond all restraint: "All right then, I slept with Ambrogio because I wanted to, simply because I wanted to! And I stopped sleeping with him when I didn't want to anymore! And that silly man from Nice never meant a thing to me otherwise! That's what I had to tell you!"

She threw open the window violently. Her heated face was lashed with cold rain and a gust of wind smelling of flooded soil; then she closed the shutters.

Michel had not stirred, and she felt ashamed, seeing him sitting motionless.

"And," she said, "you forced me to blurt that out all at once. I absolutely had to—"

"To reassure me," said Michel.

"Yes," she said naïvely. "I wanted you to be happier . . . are you happier?"

"Good heavens, that's hardly the word!"

He smiled; his gaze wavered, and his pallor was the only sign of any other feeling.

"You realize what you've just said to me: 'I told a lie; the chap's no longer an "understanding boy" nor a "cultivated and attractive friend"; it was only—how shall I put it?—a good affair?' Am I right?"

She couldn't find a word to say and felt herself blushing to the roots of her hair.

"That's all very well, my girl," he went on, "but who's going to prove to me that you haven't changed your tune, simply—as you say—to please me?"

Secretly she touched the folded pieces of paper in her pocket, remembering brief phrases from them: "a remedy? . . . But such an unpleasant one . . ." Michel looked at her with the air of an intolerably knowing detective.

"I shan't conceal the fact, I *want* to believe you. But don't overestimate my goodwill. My goodwill likes things to have a solid basis. It's up to you to show that you've condescended to enlist the support—if I may use the expression—of reality . . . or . . . convincing reality."

She could no longer tolerate either his jokes or his talk. Her hand crumpled the sheets of paper in her pocket and she brandished them in her closed fist. Michel, as though he had expected her gesture, seized her by the wrist and loosened her fingers one by one.

"Oh . . . give them back to me . . . they're mine," she moaned in dismay.

But she didn't try to recover her property and heard it crackle in Michel's hands like burning straw. Michel paid no more attention to her. Now that he was restored to reality and a keen awareness of his fate, the seizure of the letters and the subdued rustle of the crisp sheets were enough for him. *It's the same foreign paper,* he thought. *This time I've got what I want.* Breathing deeply, he no longer felt pain across his ribs halfway through each breath, and no longer found the words "if only" between himself and the urge to be master. He congratulated himself: *Poor Alice, I've got her, all right.*

"*Bono, bono,*" he said mechanically.

He had retreated behind the bureau, leaving the destitute Alice some distance away. Carefully he began to unfold the letters without tearing them, and sometimes he blew on the flimsy sheets, as a hunter blows on the still-warm feathers of the bird he has just shot. At last he had them under the palm of one hand and cupped his other hand as though protecting a flame against a draught.

At first, sheer greed made his face and eyes almost gay. His tense chin thrust forward the youthful chin-strap beard, clean-cut and rounded. As soon as he read the first words, he had to use his spectacles. Alice then leaned her forehead in her hands and concentrated on listening to the rain. But the rain was falling so monotonously that she stopped hearing it. Her heart and the pendulum of the strange little owl-shaped clock were beating to an irregular rhythm, a fact which amused her for a few moments: *My heart's doing triplets against the clock's quavery. . . . There's certainly an idea for Bizoute there. She would call it* "Chanson lugubre," *as everyone would, or else* "L'Meure mortelle."

She looked up and saw that Michel was reading no longer. "Have you finished?"

He turned toward her, his gaze obscured by the thick lenses.

"Yes. I've finished."

"I imagine you've come to a decision."

"I— Yes. Tell me . . . did you reply to him?"

She looked at him in sincere surprise.

"I? No."

"Why not?"

"Because I had nothing to say to him. What would I have written to him? Why should I have written to him?"

"Don't know. Emulation. Gratitude. Enthusiasm. A little competition in letter-writing. If the other letters are not inferior to these samples—"

She jumped to her feet, came up behind Michel and bent over the bureau.

"No, Michel, no! You've got the whole ugly story there. One, two, three letters . . . one, two, three weeks.

A horrible dream, but a short one. A nasty little affair like that doesn't go through any period of decline, thank goodness. And in any case, you'll find a date in one of the letters—this one, I think."

As she pointed out the letter her finger alighted by chance on a crude word, and before she could remove her hand or cry out Michel seized it, twisted it and pushed it away.

She rubbed her injured hand in silence, needing no explanation. As Michel tore the thin sheet into small pieces, she thought, like some disappointed philanthropist, *It really wasn't worth it. You tear yourself apart in the hope of sorting things out, and that's your reward. I shan't do it again!* As the pain in her twisted fingers subsided, she became more severe toward herself: *I've done what I suppose one must never do. I've shown him the kind of lovemaking I like, the other kind of lovemaking I like. But there's nothing more to be said now. Will he recover more quickly than from some injury to emotional pride? He promised me he would. He's said it often enough, that if only. . . .*

She shook her numb hand and sat down opposite her husband again. He had taken off his spectacles and was tearing up the other two sheets of paper with their tracery of delicate purple writing.

"Well, Michel?"

"Well, my dear. I didn't hurt your hand too much?"

She smiled and remembered Maria's laughter.

"It's practically nothing," she said. "But what about you?"

"Well, my dear," he repeated. "Well, I think that this cold shower can only—yes, it can only produce good results."

"Throw them away," she said, pointing to the fireplace.

"Indeed I will."

He burned the scraps of paper and fell silent again.

"Oh," said Alice, all at once, "listen, it's stopped raining."

"So it has," he agreed politely.

"Michel, haven't you been wondering how I came to have those letters here?"

He looked up at his wife, who found that his expression lacked either blame or an elementary, vindictive curiosity.

"Yes, I have," he replied. "I've been wondering just that. But I thought there was hardly any point . . . there was no longer any point at all in asking that question."

"You're absolutely right. Oh, Michel," she dared to say with affectionate humility, "we'll get over it without too much damage, won't we?"

She slipped down on to the floor beside him, with a languid ease that Michel called her "grass snake trick." But he recalled that one of Ambrogio's concise phrases described Alice's suppleness in another way, and mentally he began to read the three letters again, forgetting nothing, changing nothing.

They both remained thoughtful, their eyes on a dying fire where the embers were gradually turning into white ash. The gutter still hiccuped, but the drum-roll on the tiles had ceased. The wind, coming from high up and carried along by the cold river water, began to murmur, and at the same time came the unruffled voice of the rain-soaked nightingales.

"Chevestre says—" began Alice, raising one finger. "Are you surprised to hear me quote Chevestre? He says that when the rain stops at night, the morning isn't far away. Michel, what about going to bed now?"

Beneath the satin-smooth visor of her hair, her eyes, so pale in the artificial light, and slightly bloodshot, together with her swollen eyelids, made her look like a woman who's depressed after drinking. But Michel saw her resemblance to a certain Alice who used to lie happily in his arms, exhausted and silent, Alice at twenty-six who couldn't get over the thrill of experiencing pleasure. He found the strength to speak to her gently.

"Go to bed quickly. You don't mind if I stay here a little longer?"

She got up anxiously. "But, Michel . . . I'd prefer . . . if I disturb you in the bedroom . . . you know I can sleep anywhere. The divan, and my quilt—"

He interrupted her patiently.

"That wouldn't be the same thing at all, my dear. I've neglected my correspondence, and the act of writing, which I hate, will soothe my nerves and make me sleepy. Really. Go on now."

Rising regretfully, she broke up the last embers and pushed them to the back of the fireplace, then touched the bottle, which was now tepid.

"Would you like me to get some cold water, Michel?"

"This will be all right, thank you."

She drank, pulled a face, lingered still as she picked up the scattered newspapers, slipped a book under her arm, put her hand on the door handle and turned around.

"Michel, you haven't said anything to me."

She felt shy and in the grip of an unknown embarrassment.

"I'll say good night, my dear, since you're going to bed."

Seated at the bureau, with a blue pencil between his teeth, he was going through the letter rack with a self-important air.

"But tomorrow, Michel . . ."

Through his spectacles he threw her a look so piercing and so inscrutable that she paused.

"Tomorrow everything will be all right, my dear."

"All right, Michel? Do you think so?"

His look became blurred behind the convex lenses. "Better, in any case. Much better."

"That would make me so happy. Good night, Michel."

"Sleep well, my dear."

She closed the door behind her, and he listened to the closing of another door, the squeak of distant hinges. Only then did he throw down the pencil, letters, scattered papers, and walk quietly up and down. He held himself very erect, his jaws tightly clenched, and relished the freedom of entering at last, without witnesses, into a new element, one which offered slight resistance, dark in tone, somehow reddish brown in color, one where he felt certain of meeting no one. This aberration was short-lived, and when it had passed he regretted it. But he found that he could revive it by reciting certain passages from Ambrogio's three letters, and he realized that such an illusion was nothing but fury. *Fury,* he affirmed to himself. *My goodness, that's better than being miserable. How little one knows about oneself!* He stopped to drink some water and then began to walk up and down again. *I've got the energy I had at twenty, tonight.* When he intended to stop, sit down and tell himself to be calm, he was forced to begin again, raising his head and clenching his fists. As he walked, he moved his arms in time with his steps, and the gestures were not entirely voluntary. *Just what's needed for relaxation,* he thought. But he found himself aiming at the lamp and the bottle of mineral water as he went past them, wanting them to fall over and make a noise that could be heard a long way off. At the same time, he saw that his last cigarette had fallen out of the ashtray and was burning the bureau. *This worm-eaten wood is dangerous. From the attics to the cellars Cransac is worm-eaten, anyway.* In his imagination the words fire, final, flames, seemed to laugh, their f's fanning the fire and the smoke rising from it.

When all the images in red and brown, the multicolored gleams of possible broken glass faded at the same time, he sat down, cheated of his illusion. *Poor child,* he thought, *if I'd had her within reach I was capable of harming her. But what am I going to do about myself?*

He put his elbows on the desk and looked at himself absentmindedly in one of the little pocket mirrors which Alice usually left lying about. The humidity had made his hair curly, and he pushed it back from his forehead. *I don't look too bad. Except that my skin's a peculiar color. I think I look younger and better than I did yesterday. Yes, but yesterday I hadn't read Ambrogio's letters. Yesterday I wasn't very happy, it's true. But I hadn't read Ambrogio's letters. It's the whole of last week that I'd like to obliterate.*

He leafed gravely through the calendar. *Today it's . . . Tuesday. So the day after we arrived was a Monday. That Monday morning, yes, I'd gone around the mortgaged property with Chevestre. I was so anxious to get rid of him that I just left him, saying I had to telephone Paris.* He *wanted to suggest . . . what did he want to suggest to me? Oh yes, that we should build a sort of dike, an embankment, at the bottom of the vegetable garden to stop the little tricks the river plays every year.*

With the tip of his pencil he made a hole through the thin paper calendar and calculated. *In fact, if I'd followed Chevestre, if I'd even appeared to take an interest in the way the ground was slipping, if I'd come back to the house half an hour later, then perhaps nothing would have happened. It's incredible. Incredible. How much would I have now! I see myself in a straw hat, Alice bareheaded. Myself at the wheel, Alice beside me. Alice sketching the costumes for* Daffodyl*—her lip all* *blue from chewing her pencil—the face she pulls when she draws and her little nose horribly wrinkled up. Would I have all that, if I'd followed Chevestre? It's incredible. It's too much. It's too much . . .*

Tears streamed down his nose, and his weeping made him overexcited again.

"Yes, it's too much," he cried out loudly, upsetting the fragile after-midnight silence. One of the twin bookcases creaked at the end of the room and one of the glasses tinkled against the bottle of water.

On the rim of the glass a semicircle of lipstick reminded him that Alice had drunk from it. *If she were dead, I'd keep that glass,* thought Michel. *Yes, but the wide mouth that can trace a semicircle so well is living. . . . Can trace it so well . . . so well?* he repeated to himself. Three or four words came in docile fashion to complete a phrase that he had read an hour earlier, and he looked around him in alarm. *How can I escape from words like that, and from what they show me? Yet I should be able to escape. I'm not the first. Nor the last, hang it!* He regained his sang-froid, then became humble. *It's true. But I'm the only one. Like all the others. And then, the others weren't married to Alice. They haven't had all their eggs in one basket for ten years, like me. Ten years! Isn't it childish, after ten years, to get myself in a state over . . . over what, exactly? Yesterday, it was over a kind of little romance, full of confidences, shivering by the fireside, just a bit silly-silly and chatty . . .*

He pulled a face, smiled mockingly in the darkness,

and said *"pch-pch-pch-pch,"* imitating a kind of prattle.

Today, it's something else. Today. . . .

"Idiot!" he said loudly. *Idiot! I've made her suffer, and myself too, because she claimed she'd shown this man—how did she put it—friendship that was slightly physical. Trust. Is it the word "trust," or the word "friendship" that I found unbearable? It's laughable. If I could lose a day, I'd tell her, Fine! What you gave him doesn't matter at all! Give your friendship as much as you like, my child, and your trust, considering what it means to you, you women. And even if it's "slightly physical," go ahead be cheerful about it, my poor darling . . . my darling . . .*

He stifled his sobs against his sleeve, leaning his head against his folded arm.

Today I've got my deserts. If only I hadn't taken the letters from her. But I did take the letters from her, and I read them. I read them carefully. In order to prove that he had in fact read them carefully, a little phrase lifted its head in the shape of a violet-colored capital M. It looked charming for a moment, then rushed away, pulling a whole string of crude words in its wake. At the end of the letter the lover had added a precise little drawing like a flower on the train of a dress.

Michel raised his head and wiped his face. He knew that the second letter, and the third, the latter grateful and the former full of promise, were in no way inferior to the first, and that the second contained, like a great blemish, a frivolous quatrain which forced the word

"Alice" to rhyme in a scurrilous way with "calyx." His hand moved in a moderate and hopeless gesture. *It can't be sorted out. What could be worse than having no doubts? And then she might decide to take off her dress in front of me, turn her back to me as she climbs into the bathtub, go down on all fours to look for her ring or her lipstick, to . . .*

He stood up as though he'd been pushed out of his chair. *The number of crude remarks that can exist in three letters—it's unbelievable. Everything's written down, everything's described; they thought of everything, my God.*

"Everything, even what I liked best!" he shouted.

His own voice alarmed him, and he looked around. The dawn, almost as blue as moonlight, filtered through the half-closed interior shutters.

Morning already! How quickly time goes. Morning already. I was so calm. Calm isn't the right word, but I was alone. When she gets up . . . What can I do, when she opens the bedroom door? Questions, astonishment and kindhearted anxiety. And she'll tell me I'm not reasonable, and she'll come up to me, she'll put her hands on my shoulders, she, who's untouchable!—and she'll lift up her beautiful arms. What can I do now when she raises her arms, her little black armpits? And the beauty spot beside her navel? A beauty spot as big as a franc . . .

Without realizing it, he was returning, as he praised Alice, to a passionate vocabulary of the past, which they had shared, which she still allowed him to use during moments when at the sound of a word she quivered, closed her eyes and breathed in through her teeth as though it were cold. *Her beauty spot's unique! As big as a sloe. And it moved when she wanted it to. I used to say to her, "I've seen lots of women in my life, but you're the only one who's ever made eyes at me with her stomach!" Lots of women? Let's see. . . . But they didn't count, besides her.*

He lost consciousness in the middle of a word, but it was not yet time for him to rest, and the weight of his head soon woke him. He shook himself, stood up, saw that the blue gap over the window was turning white, and opened the inner shutters. Instead of the light he was afraid of, with horizontal rays across a clear sky, he found himself facing the gray dawn, the sleeping plants pulled down by their watery hair. A muted cock-crow came from inside a pen; the smell of the cowshed hung in the air, making Michel's empty stomach painfully aware of hunger. *If I eat, it's all over. I know myself.* He switched off the lamp on the bureau but didn't open the drawer that contained a revolver. *I couldn't do such a thing in my own house! Let Alice see that? And what would Maria say?*

He buttoned his jacket and felt the wallet in his pocket. *All things considered, I'll keep it, since the money's in the drawer. Let's see, now. . . . My handkerchief? Yes, I've got my handkerchief. My diary? I've got my diary. I don't think I've forgotten anything.*

In order to avoid the sound of creaking doors, he climbed over the balcony, with some difficulty. *Like a lover, Madame! A lover who's slightly stiff in the joints!*

As he brushed against the yellow jasmine and the May tree, he received a douche of raindrops so cold that he couldn't refrain from uttering a rash "Ow!" From the edge of the terrace he looked at Cransac, closed and gloomy, with its two squat towers under their deep tiled roofs. *Oh, Cransac . . . Cransac, I love . . .* He tried to rouse his emotions, but, feeling nothing, he shrugged. *No,* he admitted. *What else do I love, apart from Alice? Nothing. Cransac is like a scrap of feeling that's been preserved. And a good measure of vanity as well; come on, let's admit it. That doesn't mean that I'm leaving them both in the red, Alice and Chevestre.*

He was suddenly spiteful, like a man who's taken shelter in time and watches passersby running to escape the shower. *Oh, she'll manage all right. When she wants to. I can see her now arguing with Chevestre! And with the people from the life insurance company, who always begin by rejecting the accident theory. Oh, it'll be a fine sight. And my contract with Ambrogio! That man from Nice will find someone to talk to. She'll be magnificent; she'll have a fantastic amount of nerve. Head thrown back, cigarette in the corner of her mouth, hand on her hip.*

A sudden moment of dizziness was not enough to conceal that hip from him, nor the fold that appeared there whenever Alice was taken by surprise and turned about without freeing herself from her aggressor.

He walked briskly down the slope, crossed the thicket where it was still dark, and met the river as it lapped silently against the broken fence, its water slow-moving and heavy with iron-red mud.

Le Joutounier

As she went up the stairs, Alice felt the shape of the key in her pocket. *The same key. It's still got that twisted ring; they haven't changed it.* As soon as she had closed the door and thrown back her little crape veil, the smell of the apartment won her over again. Thirty or forty cigarettes a day, over a period of years, had given the studio a tanned look and dulled its sloping glass roof. Thirty or forty cigarette ends lay crushed in the black glass bowl, showing that the habit still persisted. *And the black glass bowl's still there! For thirty years everything here's been more or less broken, worn out, going downhill. But the black bowl's intact. But which one of them has changed her scent? Colombe or Hermine?*

She automatically pulled in her tummy in order to pass between the baby grand piano and the wall, and made contact again with the big sofa in the old way; in other words, she sat astride the upholstered back, swung herself over and let herself roll down onto the seat. But the little standard of crape which decked out her mourning hat caught on the corner of a table and remained behind. Alice wrinkled her nose and forehead angrily and got up again. In a hanging wardrobe in the part of the studio under the sloping roof she immediately found what she was looking for: a mustard-yellow suit—a plain skirt and a loose jersey tunic overprinted in green—which she sniffed. *Whom does it belong to? Hermine? Or Colombe?* Swiftly she took off her black jacket and skirt and confidently put on the jersey tunic, pulling up the zipper and tying the scarf around her neck. None of the Eudes sisters were twins, but they were all of the same build, and their tall, handsome figures were alike. In the past they had shared one suit between two of them, one hat among three, and one pair of gloves among four. . . .

This black's horrible! Alice put her clothes together, hung them in the wardrobe and looked in vain for cigarettes. *Among the three of them, they could have left me one, couldn't they?* She remembered that the three were now only two. Bizoute, the youngest, had absentmindedly got married and was making documentary films, with a vague story line, somewhere near the Marquesas Islands. Her husband was cameraman: Bizoute produced the scenes with native extras. They were kept going, just, by a sleeping partner who was dogged by bad luck, and they led a wandering life of sun-drenched poverty, moving from schooner to cargo boat, from "South Seas paradise" to "island of dreams," as could be seen from a piece of cardboard fastened to the pipe above the unlit stove, covered with snapshots: Bizoute on an atoll, Bizoute dressed in a grass skirt, wearing a crown of tiara flowers on her flowing hair, Bizoute brandishing a fish. . . . *She's thin, naturally. It's all so terribly sad. If only I'd been there. She would go and get married while Michel and I were away. It must have been a day when the cupboard was particularly bare, and crumbs of tobacco in their pockets. Bizoute, so beautiful, hitched to that dried-up Bouttemy man. Stupid girl. . . .*

On the desk, pocked with small round burns, Alice found the big box of matches underneath scraps of melodies noted down by Colombe. She shook the little wads of ash crushed between the sheets of manuscript music, found one cigarette—just one, slightly squashed—and a black cherrywood pipe: *Father's pipe!* Her hand went around the egg-shaped bowl of the pipe and she raised it to her nostrils. *Poor father . . .* Two small tears rose to her eyes; she shrugged. *He's resting. No more singing lessons, no more piano lessons. He really thought he would never have any rest. Colombe's carrying on.*

Finally she abandoned herself to the "native toutounier," a huge, indestructible sofa of English origin, battered down like a forest road in the rainy season. The back of Alice's neck encountered a cushion whose leather cover was as cold and soft as a cheek. She sniffed the old morocco which smelled of tobacco and the scent of hair, and kissed it lightly.

Who sleeps here? Hermine, or Colombe? But now they've got so much room, perhaps nobody sleeps on the toutounier anymore? She reached down between the back and the seat, felt all along the upholstery and found crushed tobacco, some transparent cellophane screwed up into a ball, a pencil and an aspirin tablet, but no pajamas rolled up into a sausage shape. Then she remained motionless, listening to the fine rain pattering on the glass. *If it weren't raining I'd air the place a bit. But I can still hear rain. Who's going to be back first, Hermine, or Colombe?*

The name and image of Michel came to torment her. She harbored against her dead husband a grudge which often distracted her from her variable, capricious and ill-controlled grief. She thought about Michel without sudden floods of tears, without any bitter abandon. But the fugitive who had been found in the water below the dam at Sarzat-le-Haut, the man who had rashly ventured as far as the river in spate, at the boundary of his property, still earned from Alice almost as much severity as regret. As she lay on her back, her lips closed over her split cigarette that failed to draw, Alice saw once again in her mind's eye the dead man who had hardly been in the water, Michel, pale and rested, his hair curly because it was wet. She was not horrified by this reticent dead man, this clumsy creature who had not taken care to avoid the heavy reddish mud. But she could find no forgiveness within herself.

The sudden slip on the smooth wet river bank led to another invisible shore. *To do that to me, Michel. . . .* Surprise, easy escape without illness or discomfort —she refused, whenever she was alone, to accept them.

As her eyes strayed over the yellowed walls, they

dwelt on familiar sketches, little pictures without frames. A large, discolored, flaky patch, behind the pipe rising from the stove, indicated the way the heat traveled.

And suppose Hermine doesn't come back? Nor Colombe either? A conjecture so absurd made her smile. The sound of the fine rain, the sand against the glass, led the traveler to the verge of sleep, and she jumped at the sound of the bent key turning in the lock.

"Hermine," she called out.

"No. It's Colombe."

Alice sat up with a twist of her back.

"You didn't cough, so I thought it was Hermine. If you must overthrow every tradition! For God's sake, have you got any cigarettes?"

A packet of cigarettes fell on to her knees. The two sisters exchanged kisses, on their foreheads and the tips of their ears, only after they had inhaled and breathed out their first puffs of smoke.

"What a filthy habit," said Colombe. "Well? So here you are! But I say, I say, don't I recognize that fabric?" She felt the mustard-colored skirt.

"Oh, it's your skirt, is it? You can have my mourning in exchange, if you want."

They began to use the "toutounier style" again, which was the way they described their inveterate liberty to tell jokes without laughing, to avoid no subject of conversation, to keep their sang-froid in almost any circumstances, and to refrain from tears.

"How's Hermine?" asked Alice.

"She's well . . . more or less."

"Is she still taken up with Monsieur Weekend?"

"Yes."

"But . . . is it the same one?"

"Definitely. Hermine's such a duffer that if she changed her man you'd be able to tell from her face. You won't find people more monogamous than us anywhere."

"No," said Alice in a mournful voice.

Colombe made her excuses by giving her sister's shoulder a caress as brief as a smack. "Sorry! I'll be careful. Tell me, did I do the right thing, not going . . . down there?"

"To Michel's funeral? Oh yes, it was the right thing. Oh!"

She flattened the leather cushion with her fist. Her impatient hand divided the thick, stiff fringe of black hair on her forehead, and her pale eyes, which became greener at the slightest trace of emotion, threatened everything that she had just left in an ill-disposed province, even the man who rested, indifferent now, in a little village cemetery at the end of a pathway bordered by apple trees in blossom.

"Oh, Colombe, that funeral! The rain that never stopped, the look in people's eyes, that curé I'd never seen before, and the people, hundreds of people, a mass of people whom I'd never seen either, in seven years. You know, when you touch the top of an anthill with your foot, and they come out everywhere. The way they looked at me. . . . I was almost charged as guilty, you know!"

She looked deeply into Colombe's eyes and let her anger subside. Her chapped lips quivered, like her nostrils. Weakness, even momentary, was ill-suited to her irregular, bold face, with its slightly crushed look and the eyes shaped like willow leaves.

"Tt, tt, tt," Colombe reproached her.

"And then," Alice went on, "on top of that, there was this . . . accident, this surprise. Nobody dies so stupidly, Colombe, you know! Nobody falls into the water like a halfwit, or at least you swim! Can't Southerners swim, then? Oh, I don't know what I'd do to him!"

She flung herself backward suddenly and smoked furiously.

"I like you better that way," said Colombe.

"So do I," said Alice. "And yet up to now I'd thought of a widow's grief as something different . . ."

Irony immediately made her look as though she were laughing. How often had this laughing look made Michel feel that his male dignity, as he called it, was being attacked?

Colombe raised her long eyebrows toward her wavy black hair, which was parted above her left temple. A single tress went across her forehead and was fixed, like a curtain, behind her right ear. The rest of her thick hair—all four Eudes daughters had this springy hair—lay over the nape of her neck in a mass of big curls.

"Maria was the only one who came to my help. Maria, yes, the housekeeper. She was wonderful. Such tact, a kind of concealed pity, I could feel it."

"But that was a new development, Alice! You always

told me that Maria was a sly old thing who was on Michel's side!"

"Yes. A typical housekeeper 'for gentlemen only.' Well, things changed, even before he died. He must have annoyed her, I don't really know how. She could see through walls, that one! She slept close to me, in the drawing room. Me on one sofa, she on the other, wearing a nightdress like a nun's."

"In the drawing room? Why in the drawing room?"

"Because I was frightened," said Alice.

She raised her long arm and let it fall on her sister's shoulder.

"Frightened, Colombe. Really frightened. I was frightened of everything—of the empty house, frightened when anyone let a door bang, frightened when it got dark. Frightened of the way . . . the way Michel went . . ."

Colombe's intelligent gaze looked right into her sister's eyes.

"Really? Do you think so?"

"No," said Alice firmly. "But it's possible," she added in a low voice.

"Problems? Business?"

Alice didn't look away.

"Oh well. There are moments when the life of a man and a woman together seems to me something slightly shameful rather like a washroom in a cupboard. It's only fit to be hidden. The proof is that I was frightened of everything that had seen us at Cransac. The two black bookcases at the end of the drawing room. The nightingales that sang all night long—oh yes, all night. That box where they had put Michel . . . and then, I was frightened of the disappearance of the box. Oh, I hate dead people, Colombe. They don't belong to the same species as us. Am I shocking you? A man . . . like that . . . well, without life: is he really the same as the one you've loved? You can't understand . . ."

With a conspiratorial hand Colombe touched the lackluster wood of the baby grand. Alice grew calm again and smiled.

"Very well. I see. I see that it's still going on, the Balabi and you. Good friends? Or good lovers?"

"What else could we be, except good friends? We're dropping from overwork, both of us." She yawned, then suddenly brightened. "But it does seem that things are looking up a little for him. He's going to conduct the musical comedy at Pouric, after the summer holidays."

She lowered her voice in order to confide to Alice, in a tone of greed and hope. "His wife's ill!"

"No?"

"Yes, my dear! And seriously. She's losing the use of her legs, and it looks as if the injections she's having don't help. Her heart could give out any moment, and then, that's it!"

She broke off, contemplating something happy and invisible, the sight of which rejuvenated her tired cheeks and the creased eyelids over her nearsighted eyes.

"But, you know, one shouldn't get excited like that.

Poor Carrine . . . he looks awful. It's mostly due to lack of sleep. We never sleep enough. We're too tired; we haven't got the heart to go to sleep. I do bits of orchestration for him, or transcriptions, whatever I can, after my lessons."

She became suddenly younger and opened her beautiful tired eyes wider: "Oh, you know, Maurice Chevalier has taken one of his songs. Just think! And do you know, except for the refrain, I wrote it. It's nice . . ." She tried to reach the keyboard behind her, stretching over the back of the sofa, but gave up: "Alice, maybe I'm not talking to you enough about . . . about what's happened to you . . ."

"Oh yes, quite enough," said Alice coldly.

Their eyes, which were almost alike, met. They concealed the pleasure they felt in being so alike, so hard on themselves; they were outwardly shameless, by inclination and from an inner modesty.

"I can hear Hermine," said Colombe. "I'll open the door for her."

With an ease that came of long practice she threw her legs over the back of the sofa and landed on her feet.

"Come in, you. Yes, Alice is here. Kiss her and then let us go on talking."

Hermine tossed her hat on the piano and slipped down beside her sisters. She leaned her own thin cheek against Alice's, and the bleached fair hair. Affectionately she closed her eyes.

"You smell good, little girl," said Alice. "Stay where you are."

"What were you saying to each other?" asked Hermine, without opening her eyes.

"Oh, nothing very remarkable, you know. I was saying that I'd had just about enough, with everything that happened down there."

All three fell silent. Alice stroked the imitation golden hair. Colombe drummed with her fingers on the resonant, once-polished wood of the Pleyel. As Alice sighed, Hermine sat up and scrutinized her sister's face.

"No, no. I'm not crying!" protested Alice. "I'm worn out. I'm thinking about all that. Poor Michou, he'd paid the insurance . . ."

"What insurance?"

"A thing, a life insurance. The insurance company wasn't nice to me, either. Suspiciously polite. An inquiry, children; they carried out an inquiry! I can tell you, I went through quite a lot down there, in more than one way. Well, it was settled, finally. And Lascoumettes, yes, Lascoumettes, you know . . . the chap who lives at the mill! He came out with it: he wants the house and the land around it! He can have them. Oh God, yes, he can have them! If I'm the only one to say he can't!"

"So," said Colombe slowly, "so you're going to have some money, then?"

"I've got some already. I'll have the insurance, the proceeds from the sale of the property—something like . . . two hundred and eighty-five thousand francs, girls."

"It's fantastic. So," said Colombe in the same dreamy voice, "so would you be able to give me—could you give me five hundred francs?"

"There you are," said Alice, fumbling in her handbag. "You silly thing, did you need it as much as that?"

"Almost," said Colombe.

She coughed in order to preserve appearances, lowered her eyes, and rubbed the inside corners of her eyes with her two index fingers. Alice almost softened as she looked at her sister's beautiful ravaged features, then remembered in time that their individual code forbade the display of emotion. She threw her arms around her sisters' shoulders.

"Come on, children! Come with me; we'll have dinner, and drink something. Stop me from thinking that Michel won't come to join us for dessert, my dear old Michel, my Michel who's silly enough to be dead . . ."

"Tt, tt, tt," said Colombe critically.

Alice heard without protest this reminder of the convention of frivolity, silence and irony that governed their relationship. But she wavered for a moment and tightened her double embrace.

"Children, I'm here. After all, I'm here," she whispered in a composed voice.

"It's not the first time," said Colombe coldly.

"Not the last, I imagine," interjected Hermine.

Alice pushed the blond head away in order to see her sister more clearly. On the collar of her close-fitting black dress Hermine had pinned a gold brooch, a rose. On one of its petals shone a diamond dewdrop.

"Oh, that's pretty!" cried Alice. "Did Monsieur Weekend give it to you?"

Hermine blushed. "Naturally. Who else?"

"But I don't want anyone else for you! I'm perfectly satisfied with Monsieur Weekend!"

"Such a good boss," insinuated Colombe.

Hermine put on a brave face and glared at her sister.

"He's up to Carrine's standard, you know. Without trying very hard."

Alice stroked the golden head of the sister who had chosen to be blond.

"Leave her alone, Colombe. She's twenty-nine. She knows her own business. Hermine, Colombe's Balabi is a very nice old *zog* . . ."

"A silly thing like me," sighed Colombe.

"Yes, but a heart of gold."

"Hey, be careful what you're saying," said Colombe, offended.

"But I don't see why Monsieur Weekend shouldn't display many of those sterling qualities which—"

"Which set you against a man," concluded Colombe. "Personally, I've nothing against Monsieur Weekend. Unless he's over eighty."

"Or covered with spots."

"Or very fair-haired."

"Or an officer on active service . . ."

"Or a conductor. We have the right to only one conductor among the four of us. Hermine, are you listening? Hermine, I'm talking to you."

Hermine was looking down, chipping off nail varnish with her thumbnail. The fair hair sufficed to reduce her resemblance to Alice, in spite of the slightly flattened nose, the family Annamite nose. A little gleaming tear furrowed its way down her fleshy nostril, shone as it hung on her upper lip, and was lost in the dark dress.

"Hermine!" cried Alice indignantly.

Hermine bent her head a little lower. "Lend me your handkerchief," she faltered.

"Leave her alone; she's crazy," said Colombe disdainfully. "You can't say anything to her. Either she makes a scene, or she cries."

"Leave her alone yourself. In any case, she must have some worry. She's thin."

She felt Hermine's upper arm, then took hold of her breast, pressed it in her hand and felt its weight.

"Not full enough," she said. "What does Monsieur Weekend do with you, then? Doesn't he give you anything to eat?"

"Yes, he does," whimpered Hermine. "He's very kind. He's given me a raise. Only, you know . . ."

"What?"

"He's married."

"He too!" cried Alice. "Do you like only married men, then, you two? And you're his mistress, naturally!"

"No," Hermine said into her handkerchief.

Colombe and Alice exchanged a glance over the bent head.

"Why not?"

"I don't know," said Hermine. "I restrain myself. Oh, it's all getting on my nerves! And Colombe's silly jokes, on top of everything."

"We're nervy," said Colombe in an affected tone of voice. "Chaste and nervy."

"Listen to her!" cried Hermine. "She says that as though she were saying I'd got lice! After all, I can do want I want! And if I'm nervous, what's that got to do with you?"

She hunched herself up in her tight black dress, raised her shoulders and crossed her arms over her breasts. At the same time she uttered violent recriminations, speaking bitterly and with strong feeling. Alice was astonished.

"Good heavens, my dear, can't you take it in good part? This isn't the first time we toutounier girls have ragged each other on the old toutounier sofa. Nobody said you couldn't do what you want! You're like the little bat I once caught in a butterfly net."

She was silenced by her own yawn.

"Oooo, let's eat. Just anything, but let's eat! It's ten past nine! Isn't there anything to eat here?"

"I was thinking of fixing eggs with ham," suggested Colombe.

"Not that. We've got fifteen years of ham and eggs to forget about. I'm taking you to Chez Gustave. What I need is a sausage as thick as my arm. Are Gustave's sausages still as yummy as ever?"

"Not really," said Hermine.

"Don't listen to her!" Colombe protested. "They're fat as butter and they melt in your mouth . . ."

"Have you finished?" Alice cut in. "I fancy Gustave and the grub. Be quick now. I'm in charge! Colombe, have you got a *tricbalous* to go with your mustard outfit?"

"I've got a little green knitted skullcap. It's wonderful; seventeen francs."

"Alice, you're not going out like that?" asked Hermine in alarm.

Alice looked at her harshly. "Why do you ask? Because I've left off the black? Yes, I've left all the crape in the glory-hole."

She stretched out her arm toward the wardrobe. "I'll put it on again in the morning."

"Doesn't it worry you? Because of . . ."

"Because of Michel? No. It doesn't upset him either, I'm sure." She stopped and shook her head. "Come on. That's my problem."

They squashed into the narrow bathroom, pulling in their stomachs and pushing out their sterns in order to pass between the washbasin and the zinc bath which had been repainted ten times over, and relaxed in idle chatter. One after the other they refurbished the red on their lips and the orange on their cheeks, pulled faces in an identical manner to ascertain the whiteness of their teeth; in fact, they resembled one another in a commonplace, striking way. But they ceased to resemble one another as soon as they put on three different hats. Colombe and Alice apparently did not notice a second little gold rose pinned into the black velvet beret topping Hermine's golden hair. All three made the same unfailing gesture, each one pulling down over her right eye the beret, the worn felt, the green woolen cap. Since Colombe had no mustard-colored coat, Alice tied a big purple scarf around her neck. While dressing, they achieved their effects with virtuosity, through a masterly use of colors and fabrics brought together in chance combinations.

"Colombe, do you remember Father's scarf, the mottled one? It suited me so well."

All three smiled at one another in the tarnished glass. Before going downstairs they exchanged the ritual words.

"What about the *busette?*"

"It's still in the lock. I'll take it. And the *sisibecques?*"

"We pass a tobacconist's," said Alice; "I'll buy some for everyone."

They walked arm in arm, talking loudly, across the deserted street, breathing in the damp twilight. Alice pushed open the door of Gustave's restaurant with her foot, like an habituée. She drifted as far as the table she liked best, by an open fireplace, and sat down with a sigh of pleasure. The long room, in the depths of a thick-walled old Parisian building, stifled noise. Nothing had ever been sacrificed to any personal taste or to any refinement.

"You see," said Colombe, "it's unchangeable. You come here to eat, just as you go to a confessional to confess."

"Even a confessional allows itself some decorations and carvings in temporal taste. Where's Hermine?"

Hermine had lingered by a table to talk to a woman

dining alone who was simply dressed and a little dumpy.

"Who's that female?" asked Alice.

Colombe put her lips to Alice's ear. "Madame Weekend. The real one. The legal one."

"Really?"

"Yes. Her name's Rosita Lacoste."

"But what about him, the man we call Monsieur Weekend? Is he called . . ."

"Well now, he's called Lacoste. Not at business; his business is called Lindauer."

"Colombe, what do you think he'll do with the child?"

Colombe shrugged.

"There's no reason why he shouldn't marry the child someday. As if one only married bachelors! But there are a lot of things I don't know. Hermine has changed, as you've seen."

"And suppose I ask her point blank?"

"I don't think that's a very good idea. Be careful; she's coming."

"What are you going to eat, little one? Tell me, Hermine."

"I . . . the same as you," said Hermine.

"I'm having *brandade de morue* and pork sausage," said Alice.

"I'm having a minced beef thing with an egg on top of it and raw onion all around," said Colombe. "And *crème au chocolat* after the cheese."

"Champagne nature, or beaujolais, Hermine? Hermine! Come back!"

"I'm cold," said Hermine, rubbing her hands together. "A pepper steak *au poivre* and salad."

"Cold? In this weather? The eighth of May? Colombe, did you hear what she said?"

Colombe replied with a gesture the younger sister could not see, and Alice said no more.

"Drink something, Hermine; you'll feel warmer."

They emptied their first carafe of wine before eating. Alice was breathing more deeply and the nervous tightness in her ribs had relaxed. The wine and the need to eat brought her to a state of well-being, and all the lights seemed to her to glow a brighter yellow.

The faces of her two sisters opposite suddenly lost the characteristics imposed by unseeing habit and turned into unknown faces, like those encountered only once, that have nothing to hide. Colombe did not conceal her thirty-four years and fed her chronic tracheitis with nicotine.

A beautiful face, thought Alice. *She has commas at the corners of her mouth, lips like mine, but they've become thinner through gripping her cigarette while reading, playing the piano, singing, talking. She looks at you like some honest person who's lost all hope. There are long furrows down her cheeks. I bet she's never made eyes at anyone except the Balabi, another example of pure virtue and fidelity. Little Hermine's very pretty, in spite of her fair hair, or because of it. But there's something wrong somewhere. Is it a health problem? Or worries? Jealousy? This Monsieur Weekend business isn't clear. Why has the other Madame Weekend come here? It's wonderful to be here with my toutounier girls, and the brandade is like velvet.*

She drank another glass of cool, fruity wine, and the roar of the sea arose in her ears. Her well-being increased as a result, disturbed only by a vague worry, something black like a smoky ceiling or a low, trailing cloud. She wrinkled her forehead and wondered what it could be. *Oh yes,* she said to herself, *I know what it is: Michel's dead. He's dead and it's already been going on for days and days, and I wonder if it's going to go on much longer. . . . What are they scrapping about now, those two?*

"No, I haven't been," Hermine was saying.

"I know that very well," said Colombe.

"Precisely. I haven't been; it's no secret."

"It's no secret, but you didn't tell me. You told me, 'I have to wait,' trying to make me believe that it was the theatre management asking you to wait until the girl at the box office had left. While I, like a willing horse, I was cutting myself in two to make sure that no one else got the job. You could have told me quite simply that it didn't interest you, that you didn't need an extra thousand francs a month—and I congratulate you on it."

"In the first place, I hadn't asked you to do anything!"

Hermine had not raised her voice but assumed once again her peevish, victimized expression; she looked contemptuously at Colombe, and uttered a hoarse little groan at the end of every sentence. Colombe treated her without acrimony but wore her down until she gradually became exasperated. Alice made an effort to emerge from her buzzing, bright yellow world.

"Now, now, what's all this? No arguments while we're eating: Paragraph three of the Code Toutounier. Paragraph four: Never have arguments in public."

"Everyone's gone," said Colombe.

"Hermine's woman's still there. She's paying her bill."

"She won't have indigestion; she had a cocktail," observed Colombe.

"Who is that stout person?" asked Alice casually.

"A former dress designer for Vertuchou, I think," Hermine replied in the same way. "I met her at the Epinay studio when I was an extra in *Her Majesty Mimi.*"

"Is she with Vertuchou?"

"She was, I believe. I don't know whether she is now. Give me something to drink. I've got such a thirst. . . ."

She diluted her wine with water, and the neck of the carafe trembled against the rim of the glass. Alice looked at the gray-haired woman who had now reached the door. Hermine stopped eating and put her knife and fork down on her plate.

"Not hungry anymore?"

"Not really."

"Pity. Shall we have a different wine, Colombe?"

"A drop of beaujolais, to go with the cheese."

Colombe's cheekbones and the sides of her nose were becoming slightly red. One of her eyes was half-closed due to her habitual smoking, and she sat drumming with her fingers on the edge of the table. Alice was not surprised that neither of her sisters talked to her about Michel. She herself, assailed from time to time by that frozen memory, repulsed the dead man's entreaty as though he were waiting for her at home. "Soon . . . just be patient . . ." He was no longer a body that had been fished out of the water, wet and horizontal. Perhaps he was in the house, sitting there with the telephone to his ear, or standing, his elbows on the high desk at the Tronchin office. "Just a moment, Michel. . . . Leave us alone. . . . You know very well that for us Eudes girls this is our relaxation, these little meals where we don't want any guests . . ."

"Will you have some fruit, Hermine? Or the *tarte maison?*"

"No, thank you."

"Is something wrong?"

"Everything's perfectly all right."

And to prove it, Hermine pushed her plate away, pressed her napkin to her eyes, and sobbed violently.

"Hermine!" cried Colombe.

"Leave her alone. It'll be over more quickly if she doesn't hold back."

Alice began to eat again, followed by Colombe, who was blossoming once more under the beneficial influence of red meat and honest wine; in addition, she was comforted and as though cured forever of all worries by the large five-hundred-franc note folded up in her handbag.

Fraternal shame made them turn away from the affected sister, and they refrained from looking at her as though she had been afflicted by stomach pains or nosebleeding in public. Hermine became calmer, wiped her eyelashes, and powdered her face.

"*Guézézi, guézézi,*" Alice said to her in encouraging tones.

Hermine's light-colored eyes, which seemed blue now that she was blond, glittered below their smarting lids.

"*Guézézi,*" she repeated. "It's easy enough to say it. You've got to be able to."

She asked for some early cherries, gathered far away from Paris and already withering on their dried-up stems. At the edge of the wood, by the water, the cherries were still in flower, Alice remembered. *On Michel's wet hair there were two or three petals from the cherry tree . . .* She knitted her brows, glared unkindly at the landscape that was coming to life again, and at its innate skill and mysteriousness, and applied her entire defensive strength to observing her younger sister.

Hermine was still pale and upset, absentmindedly squeezing her cherry stones between her thumb and forefinger. With apprehension and a kind of repugnance, Alice thought that she might have to force her secretive fair-haired sister to break her silence. *Is she secretive? We've made a point of hiding our problems from one another ever since we were children.* They had never known internal strife, nor family rivalry. Their struggles were of another kind. The struggle to eat, to find a post as designer, saleslady, secretary, accompanist in a local dive; to form among the four of them a mediocre string quartet for the big cafés. . . . Hermine had been a mannequin several times. A fine method of wasting away, of coming to the end of your strength, feeling revolted by black coffee yet searching the studios for it. And Bizoute? How pretty Bizoute was, framed in the box-office window at the Bouffes! But you soon learn, when you're one of the four Eudes daughters, about the designs formed by admiring men; they would come up against a glass wall, a bronze grill, a couturier's entrance, and hardly tried to go any further. *So much so,* thought Alice, *that I wonder if most of the so-called victims who say they were loved too much don't invent it all.*

Colombe, the musician, would not have deserted music, even during the worst weeks, for goose with chestnut stuffing. Alice herself was capable of anything. She had even been capable of getting married. Chaste lives, in fact, the lives of poor, scornful girls, dashing in their down-at-heel shoes, looking love up and down inconsiderately, as if to say, "Out of the way, old thing, stand aside. Before you, come hunger, ferocity, and the need to laugh . . ."

Alice looked secretly at Hermine, at the chin that was growing sharper, the shadow on her cheek, beneath a limp curl of fair hair. She sighed and emerged from her solitude.

"Coffee, toutounier girls?"

Colombe repulsed the temptation with a violent gesture and then accepted it with a humble laugh.

"Oh, yes, coffee! Coffee, and who cares! Coffee, calva, everything!"

She turned the menu over and rapidly wrote down some notes of music. The felt hat over one eye, and the cigarette that pulled her mouth to the right, removed from her features only the symmetry, leaving their expression of noble and absentminded fatigue untouched. *She deserves better than she's got,* Alice decided, *even counting Carrine, known as the Balabi.*

"You oughtn't to have coffee tonight, Hermine."

"Don't you think so?"

The younger sister was smiling, but Alice noticed the defiant coldness of the smile and became secretly alarmed.

"As you wish, my dear."

On the table, which had now been cleared, the gray-moustachioed waiter placed a paper cloth, calvados the color of light caramel, and steaming cups, then the earthenware pot with a filter, and Colombe became animated.

"Their coffee always smells good, doesn't it, Alice? Well? What are you planning to do after all that?"

"All what?"

"But Alice, I meant . . . well, Michel . . ."

"Oh yes. . . . Nothing. Nothing for the moment. There's still a whole lot of legal business. Oh, yes. Luckily Michel has no family. Most of all, I intend to talk about him as little as possible."

"Good. As you wish."

"Because, to be honest, I . . . I'm not very pleased with him over this business . . ."

"What business?"

"You see—I think he shouldn't have died." She stubbed out her cigarette in a saucer, and repeated, with a tentative look, "I think he oughtn't to have died. I don't know if you understand me . . ."

"Very well. I think so. You're just as severe, in fact, over a ridiculous accident as you would be over . . . over a suicide."

"Precisely. Suicide isn't very splendid."

"Whatever the reason for it?" asked Hermine.

She listened to her sisters in a state of agitation, drawing on the paper tablecloth with a sharp fingernail.

"Whatever the reason for it," said Alice.

"Whatever the reason for it," repeated Colombe. She exchanged a cool, staunch look with Alice.

"Still," said Hermine, "there are suicides caused by . . . by despair . . . love."

"That's what you say! What do you think, Alice? As for me," Colombe ventured to say, "I think that if a man loves me, he oughtn't to prefer anything else to me, not even suicide."

"But what if you'd driven him to despair, Colombe?"

Colombe looked at her sister with a kind of majestic naïvety.

"How could he be in despair if I existed? Logically he could only be in despair if I didn't exist anymore."

"I like the 'logically,'" said Alice, smiling at Colombe.

But Hermine blushed to the roots of her hair. More secretive than her sisters, she occasionally became more transparent.

"I think you're—I think you're incredible!" she cried. "You're disputing a man's right to fall into the water without doing it on purpose!"

"Naturally," said Alice.

"Oh! . . . that man who thought about what would happen to you even after he was dead, who thought of making your existence secure . . ."

"So what?" said Alice roughly. "You know what I feel about material comforts. He'd have done better to preserve his own existence."

"Oh, you're . . . you're . . ."

Hermine pulled a long strip off the paper tablecloth and, lowering her voice, uttered a few insulting words. Colombe and Alice waited for her to calm down; their very patience and reserve seemed to hurt her. When she rashly sighed, "Poor Michel!" Alice placed her hand on her arm.

"Be careful, my dear. You've drunk a little wine this evening. You're the only one of the four of us who can't take your wine. Michel is my business. Even where he is now. If I can't say what I think in front of you two, if I can't be quietly wrong, through natural unfairness, or through . . . love . . ."

Hermine impetuously freed her arm and placed her cheek against Alice's hand. "Of course you can!" she cried, keeping her voice low. "Be wrong! Be wrong! Pay no attention! You know I'm the youngest!"

"Tt-tt-tt," said Colombe critically.

"Don't scold her," said Alice.

With tender anxiety she let the warm cheek lie against her hand, and the soft untidy blond hair fell over the green and brown sleeve that she did not recognize.

"Behave yourself, child. The honest waiter's still there with that moustache that makes him look like a bath-attendant. Come on, we're going home to bed now. Colombe, are you seeing the Balabi at his place tonight?"

Colombe replied only with a sad and negative shake of her head.

"And what about you, Hermine? Are you going out?"

"No," said Hermine dully. "Where would I go?"

"Then drop me on the way. I'll pay for a taxi. I'm half asleep."

"But who've you got at your place to help you?" said Colombe.

"Tomorrow morning I'll have the daily."

"And tonight?"

"Tonight, nobody."

All three of them fell silent and got ready to go, concealing the fact that all three were thinking about the apartment that Alice was going to enter alone, and where she would spend the night alone.

"Alice," said Hermine, "are you going to keep that apartment—I mean your apartment?"

Alice raised her long arms. "You ask me that! How do I know? No, I shan't keep it. Yes, I shall keep it—for the time being. And now let's go, or I'll fall asleep on the table."

The night, misty and mild, was without breeze or scent. In the taxi Alice sat between her two sisters and put her arms through two arms like her own, and just as beautiful. But Hermine's arm she felt to be thinner; her elbow was sharp. *What can be happening to little Hermine?*

"If you should need anything," said Colombe suddenly, "Odeón 28–28."

"Have you had the telephone put in at last? That's a great day!"

"I didn't do it," said Colombe curtly. "It's in Hermine's room."

Standing on the pavement, all three of them looked up at the third floor as though they were afraid of seeing a light burning. Alice let her sisters leave and then closed the heavy door. As soon as she entered the slow-moving lift with its ornamental Gothic ironwork, she was aware of her own cowardice. The sound of a key turning in the lock, a strip of wood in the parquet floor which creaked beneath the carpet as she crossed the vestibule, other familiar creaking sounds, the same ones that had accompanied Michel when he came back at night, told her clearly that her sang-froid had deserted her. She courageously tolerated fear like any other discomfort, admitting its existence by discussing it. *I need only keep a light on all night,* she thought.

With a firm hand she opened the door of Michel's study, put all the lights on and breathed in the faint smell of leather, toilet water, tobacco and printer's ink, which brought an affectionate sob to her throat, tears of pure regret which, if she had allowed herself to shed them fully, would have brought her relief. But she suddenly noticed on the desk a pair of men's gloves in thick, sulphur-yellow pigskin, and she began to sweat slightly as she looked sideways at those yellow gloves of Michel's, their full, curved fingers assuming the attitude of a familiar, living hand. She lowered her head, forced herself to be obedient and attentive, listened to the beating of her heart, gauging her chances of spending a more or less quiet night. She reckoned also that she would inevitably encounter a pair of Michel's pajamas hanging in the bathroom, and, above all, the presence of the twin bed which would stand beside hers, empty and covered with tawny velvet. Ever since she had confronted at Cransac a Michel who was recumbent forever, she had rebelled with all her strength against the image of a bed which denied rest and pleasure; Michel's bed.

Her pride and good sense would not allow her to give way all at once, and she remained standing in the middle of the study, in front of the desk, which had the tidiness easily maintained by people who write little. In the center lay the blotter with leather corners, beside it the little hand blotter, red and blue pencils and a chromium-plated metal ruler. *A ruler,* thought Alice. *Who uses a ruler? I'd never noticed there was a ruler.*

And that ashtray. . . . How did I come to leave him that café-type ashtray? She forced a smile. But she knew very well she would give in. Her black fringe was sticking to her forehead. A breeze came across the room through the slats of the closed shutters and ruffled a piece of paper lying on the desk.

That's enough, thought Alice. A drop of perspiration ran down from her forehead. With an attempt at lucidity she banished from her brain and eyes the cloud that produces ghosts, and left the room without forgetting to switch out the lights.

She got up the staircase, which was a strain for her shaky knees. *I'm almost there . . . one more floor . . . there, that's the end.* The street was in front of her, with its midnight passersby, walking rapidly; and, overhead, the dusty stars. She smiled, feeling dead-tired, and called out mechanically: "The toutounier . . . the toutounier . . ."

On the landing outside the home apartment, she heard Colombe's voice answering Hermine's, and she knocked gently, adopting the agreed rhythm. Colombe exclaimed "Well now!" and opened the door. She was bundled up in a pair of old Eudes's pajamas. Her damp hair was brushed back from her forehead, which was whiter than the rest of her face.

"Come in, my toutounier girl! So you've come back? What's the matter?"

Alice lowered her little flat nose and tearfully pulled a face. "I was afraid, all on my own," she said, without shame. "Where does our little sister sleep?"

"In the bedroom. In the real bed. I've kept the toutounier."

Alice looked at the enormous divan, the sheets tucked in just anyhow, the dip down the middle, the evening papers on the rug that served as a blanket, and the lamp on the piano shaded for the night with a twist of blue paper.

Half an hour later she was lying in a half-conscious slumber like that enjoyed by animals. When Colombe joined her, Alice, in her sleep, unfolded one of her arms. She knew vaguely that one of her long legs, its knee bent, was lying parallel to a similar leg. An arm groped through the air and found its protective place across a breast. Colombe's mouth kissed, in haphazard fashion, smooth hair and the tip of an ear, sighed "*Guézézi, guézézi*" to ward off bad dreams, and was silent until the morning.

"Endives!—luv-erly chicoree! . . ." chanted a voice in the street. Alice listened incredulously. Part of her was awake; another part could not free itself from a dream.

Endives! It's too wonderful. I'm dreaming, thought Alice. *Or else I'm twenty-six years old, and Michel has made a date with me tonight at the little Grévin theatre.*

An arpeggio on the piano, then the recitative-preamble to *Schéhérazade* woke her up in the ritual manner. She was lying alone in the depths of the native toutounier, beneath the glass roof of the studio which was protected by a green curtain. The back of the divan united her with the baby grand, and, as in the past, she absorbed music, its vibrations spreading into her loins, her back and the airy cage of her lungs. She felt so resonant that she threw off what remained of her dream and stretched out her arms to the green daylight, the melody, the musician and the memory of herself at twenty-six.

Colombe sat at the piano smoking, one eye closed and her head tilted sideways. She had rolled the sleeves of her father's pajamas up above her elbows and was operating the pedals with her bare feet.

"Where's the other one?" called Alice.

"Making the coffee," mumbled Colombe.

She left the piano, opened the low window beneath the glass panel, and leaned out.

"Endives—luv-erly chicoree! . . ." came the chant from the street.

Alice jumped up, tightened the cord of the bathrobe in which she had slept and joined her sister.

"Colombe! It's the same woman! Colombe!"

"That's right!"

"Can a street-hawker go on hawking so long, then?"

Colombe's only reply was a yawn, and the May morning showed up her tiredness.

"Did I keep you awake, Colombe?"

A long arm fell across Alice's shoulders.

"Good heavens no, girl. But I think I'm three years behind with my sleep. And what about you? Did you have a good night? *Soun, soun, veni veni ben?* How fresh you are! I haven't looked at you so far. Alice . . . I wouldn't want to hurt you, but . . . can you really look as you do this morning and feel sad?"

Alice eased her shoulders.

"That's silly, Colombe. Some dogs die even with cold noses. Besides, there's no question of my dying. One isn't morally responsible for good health."

"On the contrary," said Colombe. "One always is, a little."

In the sunshine that reached the window Alice

blinked, screwed up her nose and raised her upper lip. Her grimace revealed her pink gums and deeply set wide teeth, while over her cap of black hair, with the fringe just above her eyebrows, played a blue gleam. Suddenly she became animated.

"Just think, Colombe. For three weeks I led an impossible life down there, without telling anyone. And the strangest thing was that I found it possible. The insurance company, Lascoumettes, the notary, everyone was against me. Even Michel. Yes, even Michel! Leaving me like that, all alone, from one moment to the next. . . . You can say what you like, but drowning yourself by accident at six o'clock in the morning is suspect. And most of all, it's unsporting. What a pack I had at my heels! What did they think? Did they imagine they would get me? That I would let the whole thing go, house and land, for nothing? So I said, We'll see. You know, Lascoumettes is someone. Yes, you *do* know him; he's a great strapping fellow who has lots of vineyards on the hillside. He wanted Cransac. Chevestre did too, naturally. But not Chevestre! It's really too awful to sell a property to one's agent. Then I invited Lascoumettes to lunch to discuss the sale. Armagnac, braised beef, a hare they'd caught in a trap. Oh, my dear, I know why widows in the country put on weight. And you know, Lascoumettes would even have married me! He would have taken everything that way—the property and the wife. Well, in the end, it was settled. Only yesterday I took a dislike to our *pied-à-terre;* I was frightened. So I came back here. This toutounier, sleeping in the same basket with you. Waking up with *Schéhérazade,* the 'luverly chicoree . . .', everything. How much I needed it, Colombe! Give me more hospitality from the time when we were broke. . . ."

She stopped, out of breath, stretched, struck the window frame with both hands and closed her eyes, which were full of sunshine and tears. Her bathrobe fell open over a breast which lacked fullness but did not sag at its base.

"To think that I used to look like that," sighed Colombe, who was admiring her. "Oh, poor Balabi. He deserves better than what's in store for him. There's hardly anything in store for him now."

She pushed back the curtain of hair from her forehead and shouted toward the bedroom at the back, "Well now, what about that coffee? It's a quarter to ten, for heaven's sake!" She lowered her voice. "Alice, do you know what Hermine's doing? She's telephoning. I could hear her at seven o'clock this morning."

"What was she saying?"

"I couldn't make out the words. But I didn't like the tone of voice. It was flat, without expression. I only heard: 'I'll explain. No. No. Not on any account.' And then tears."

They looked at each other in bewilderment. The door that separated the studio from the corridor was kicked open. Carrying a tray, Hermine came in, along with the smell of coffee and toast.

"Two white and one black!" she announced. "The concierge had only kept the milk downstairs. The butter's all soft this morning. Good morning, both of you."

As she moved between the divan and the piano, balancing the tray on the mountain of papers that covered the desk, she was as skillful and pleasant as a well-brought-up young girl. When the cups had been filled and the toast handed around, Hermine sat astride the arm of the toutounier.

"Did you sleep well, Alice?"

Alice replied with a nod and a smile. She was examining with amazement Hermine's pajamas, the Persian-type trousers in pink satin crepe, the girdle with its silk fringe, the reddish lace yoke revealing the false blonde's tawny-skinned breasts. From Hermine's bare feet hung pink mules with large silver flowers.

"What you can do with thirty-nine francs, after all," said Alice.

Hermine's little ears, pale beneath the cold blond hair, went red. She glared suddenly at her sister, collected the empty cups on the chipped lacquer tray and went out.

"I see," said Alice to Colombe, "we can't make jokes anymore. She never used to be like that. You're sure it's the same Monsieur Weekend?"

"Yes. But you might think it wasn't the same Hermine anymore. And do you think it's proper for her to know Madame Weekend? I say it's immoral for two women to know each other when they oughtn't to."

"Do you often utter imperishable remarks like that, my Colombe Noire? What on earth do you know about immorality?"

Alice's laughter expressed the kind of irreverent veneration she felt for her sister. In return, the latter showed her the profound and childish honesty of a soul which nothing could demean or embitter.

"Listen, Alice, I'll make you an offer. I'll leave you the dressing table; let me have the bathtub. I'm late."

"No bargaining! You can have everything. I'll take a bath at my place. What about lunch? Here or somewhere outside?"

The tall Colombe opened her arms wide in despair.

"Two lessons at Val-de-Grâce, and my singing class at half past two, on the far side of Auteuil. How could I . . . I pass a crémerie where they serve hot things."

"And what about Hermine?"

"Oh, she doesn't come back for lunch. Her work doesn't allow her the time, or so she says. You're going to be very solitary."

"I've lots to do, as you can imagine!" said Alice, sounding self-important in order to hide her disappointment. "Does the concierge still come up at midday? I'd like to give her some money for the housekeeping."

"You gave me some last night."

"Oh, don't. I'm taking over the financial side again. Leave it to me. I don't like the money I've got. When shall we meet?"

"On the native toutounier, half past six, seven o'clock."

"What about Hermine?"

"Don't bank on seeing her. Hermine!" she shouted

at the top of her voice, "will you be having dinner with us?"

There was no reply, but a few seconds later Hermine came in and banged the door behind her. She was in a devastating and incomprehensible state of disorder. Her silk-fringed girdle dangled loosely to the floor, the lace yoke had slipped off one of her naked shoulders, and her face showed that her makeup had been interrupted. Alice adopted Colombe's customary sang-froid and waited. The expression of violence so obvious on Hermine's features faded, and she leaned against the door.

"Have you been having a fight?" said Colombe without raising her voice.

"More or less," replied Hermine.

"Can we hear about it, or can't we?"

"You can't."

She retied her girdle and covered up her naked shoulder.

"Very well," said Colombe. "Alice was asking if you'd be having dinner with us."

"Dinner? . . . oh, yes, certainly." She added, with absentminded politeness, "With pleasure," and smiled mechanically, revealing the wide family teeth and the gums of someone suffering from anemia. Then she looked at Alice with the expression of a frightened child and went out.

"Well?" said Colombe. "Did you see that? Oh heavens, my train . . ."

"But, Colombe . . . are we going to leave her like

that? Aren't we going to try to find out . . . to help . . . I don't recognize the girl anymore."

Colombe tilted her head, half-closed one eye to avoid her cigarette smoke and shrugged.

"You can always try. I give up. These stories about Monsieur Weekend, telephone calls, divorce, and even anonymous letters . . . oh, I don't know. . . ."

She flexed her nicotine-stained muscular fingers, skilled at touching the keyboard and plucking strings.

"Anonymous letters?" said Alice quickly. "Who to?"

"Perhaps Hermine has received some too," said Colombe hesitantly. "Once she had to go—"

"Go? Where? Who made her, where?"

"He's a kind of special commissioner, I think. It's where you go to lodge complaints about family quarrels and—well—blackmail. . . ."

"But it wasn't Hermine who lodged a complaint? Tell me about it—have I got to drag it all out of you?"

"I don't know much about that sort of thing, you know."

"When was it?"

"Let me think . . . January."

"So she was suspected, then," said Alice after a silence. "But of what?"

"I don't know," said Colombe sincerely. "All I know, that is, what I'm telling you, it came afterward, a bit at a time—things I heard said over the telephone, things I worked out for myself. You can see she's quite unapproachable. Oh, my goodness, my train, my two kids waiting for their lesson . . ."

Alice went out without seeing her younger sister again. Unusual modesty kept Hermine in the only bedroom, where the door was bolted. "You can't come in," she shouted through it. "I'm naked and tattooed all over! Yes, my sweet, dinner tonight! *Guézézi, guézézi!* And we'll go to the cinema afterward! Yes, my sweet!"

Alice lost patience and left, wearing black, with her little crape veil over her nose.

Without premeditation she took the familiar route. Her long stride carried her safely along as it had in the past when, after an innocent toutounier orgy of chatter, silence and smoking, she would return to her husband and their *pied-à-terre.* Mirrored in a shop-window, she saw coming toward her a tall woman in mourning who held her head high as she walked and seemed to be moving in time to music.

Oh, my dress is rather short, she decided. Black stockings emphasized the shape of long, aristocratic legs. She heard Michel's pleasant voice: "Where are you off to in those clothes, you interminably tall creature?"

The memory was so strong that she bumped into a café table and bruised her big toe. She had not imagined that Michel's absence, Michel's death and her own grief would take so long to establish themselves within her, to reach a constant level, a certainty that neither sleep nor activity could disturb. What chaos. And how could she describe it? Sometimes there would be a sudden moment of total, obtuse forgetfulness of her loss: "I must have a lining made for my summer coat." At which point memory would return violently and the blood would rush to Alice's cheeks. Then there would be moments of total ingratitude which came from far away, developing without effort, the indifference of a woman who might never have had a husband, or a lover, or known Michel, or wept over a man's death.

In the first place, you don't weep for a man who's dead; you forget him, or you replace him, if you don't die yourself from his absence! During these furtive periods of dried-up feeling, she tried to be ashamed of herself, but another, more knowing Alice was not unaware that a woman is ashamed only of what she lets others see, not of what she feels. . . .

Oh, kingcups from damp fields—they're so beautiful . . . She was already opening her handbag to buy a spray of big kingcups, yellow and shiny, which had grown in running water; but she thought of her concierge, and of the daily, people with rigid principles. *Perhaps I should respect those ladies' feelings and buy nothing but dyed everlasting flowers? I'll teach them, I will . . .*

However, she suffered them, one after the other, with resignation. While she was waiting in the dark for the lift to come down, she heard words of disapproval from the concierge's room. "A short little veil like that, I tell you it's barely good enough to wear when you've lost an uncle!" The daily woman, a faceless servant who came and went intermittently, gazed insistently at Alice in the hope of finding the white widow's band on her forehead and black cotton gloves on her hands. Her solicitude showed in one single question:

"Wouldn't Madame like me to make her a little herb broth?"

Alice nearly burst out laughing. But her untimely gaiety did not last long. In the conjugal apartment, where all the windows were wide open to the May sunshine, she felt bitter and intolerant. She searched about her in vain for the fear she had felt the previous day and the wandering presence of a disembodied Michel. *I wanted to sort papers. What papers? I know what Michel's files are like; they're all in order. There's the file for the management of the Omnium cinema at Saint-Raphaël, the one for the Théâtre du Mail in Montpellier, the one for the Jalerie Plumes and Pinceaux in Lyon, the one for the Mediterranean tour. There are the disastrous Cransac accounts . . . the accounts of a poor little life; he was short of money, rather superficial, fairly hardworking; he was often at the bottom of the hill while I was going up it. As for me, I've got my sketches here, costume designs for* Queen Eleanor. *I've got two dresses, two coats . . .* She leaned against one of the windows, looking out over the street without shops. *I don't want anything here. I don't like anything, I don't condemn anything. . . . Where does it hurt?*

"Is Madame going to have lunch here this morning?"

Alice turned around quickly: "No, I'm lunching with my sisters, you see . . ."

She paused, suddenly disheartened in a way that seemed strange to her; but the woman apparently found it quite natural, for she nodded her head with its lifeless hair and raised a hand:

"I quite understand! . . . And will Madame be eating here this evening?"

Alice had expected the question, but she jumped all the same.

"No. I'm better when I'm with my sisters at the moment. I'll sleep there too. By the way, I won't have the telephone connected again. Is the water hot? I'll take a quick bath."

A quarter of an hour was enough. In spite of the hot water she was shivering. She didn't touch the beige pajamas that hung in the bathroom, awaiting Michel's return, and she carefully removed the toothbrush which lay next to Michel's in a little coffin-shaped opaline case. Then she filled a suitcase, threw a black coat over her arm, and in order to be certain there was nothing to keep her there, she held the door wide open while she made the daily responsible for the upkeep of the apartment.

I tolerate the fact that Michel's dead, and I weaken over things of no importance, in front of people without personal spite, although there's no proof that the daily hasn't got any personal spite. The toutounier . . . quick, the toutounier . . .

She closed her eyes affectionately. *The toutounier. . . . The hideout, the cave, with its signs of humanity, its humble marks against the walls, its untidiness which isn't dirty. No one's been very happy there, but no one wants to leave it. . . .* She remembered that she was lunching alone and felt no desire for any restaurant. On her way back to the studio she bought some fresh fennel, a tin of tuna fish, new-laid eggs, cream cheese, and a quarter bottle of champagne. But the imperious hunger that gnawed at the pit of her stomach disorganized her snack. While one egg was dancing about in the boiling water, Alice ate the tuna fish without bread, sprinkled pepper on the cheese, and chewed the fennel as dessert without realizing that she had not opened the little bottle of champagne. She put it away in cupboard No. 2, which was in the kitchen. On the sink, a pair of silk stockings was soaking in an enamel basin.

Are they Colombe's stockings, or Hermine's? Hermine's, I imagine; they're sheer. She washed them quickly and laid them over a small towel. She hummed to herself, her cigarette firmly clasped between her lips. *And what about coffee? I forgot the coffee! I'll go and have some across the road.*

She went into the bedroom where Hermine slept. *It's rather untidy, but it smells nice.* She put away a pair of shoes, the satin crepe pajamas and a large comb. The dull light that came from a small courtyard looked more cheerful through pink curtains with black flowers. *It's smarter than when our father was here,* thought Alice. *But I like the studio better. This bedroom's like Hermine, full of things I don't know.*

Singing to herself, "*coffee, heartening potion . . . ,*" she put on the little black hat again and went downstairs. On the second floor, a woman who was running up the stairs bumped into her and apologized breathlessly.

"Hermine!"

"Yes—"

"What's the matter?"

"Nothing. Do you mind? I'm going up."

Hermine stumbled and Alice put her arm firmly around her. The little black beret with its gold rose brooch fell to the ground; Hermine did not bend down to pick it up.

"I'll come up with you. Hold on to the rail," said Alice. "Hold on to the rail, I tell you."

She groped on the floor for the velvet beret, let her sister into the studio and pushed her on to the leather divan. The only strange things about Hermine, who was bareheaded now, her fair hair falling over her forehead, were her pallor and the way her eyes moved incessantly from right to left, as though she were reading.

"Have you been drinking?" asked Alice.

Hermine shook her head.

"Have you been eating? Neither? You're not hurt?"

She quickly picked up her sister's handbag, but found no weapon in it.

"Wait a moment."

She brought the little bottle of champagne and half-filled a glass.

"Here. Yes, yes, drink it. Tepid champagne is the ideal emetic. What's happened, my child?"

Hermine moved the glass away from her moist lips and glared at her sister.

"I'm not your child! I've fired at Madame Lac . . . Madame Weekend!"

"What!"

"I've fired at Madame Weekend! How many times do I have to say it?"

She emptied the glass and put it down. Alice lowered her head and rubbed her fingers, which felt stiff, cold and itchy.

"Is—is she dead?" she asked.

Hermine shrugged her shoulders furiously.

"Of course not! I'm much too clumsy! No, she's not dead. Not even wounded!"

"But people know . . . Are they going to arrest you? Hermine, is it true what you're telling me? My dear 'Mine—"

Hermine began to cry, whimpering like a child.

"No, they won't come and arrest me. I missed. She laughed at me. She said I could come home, that she wouldn't even lodge a complaint . . . that I was only an idiot. She also said I was living on romantic stories—oh, Alice . . ."

She pressed her fists to her eyes in a rage.

"Weren't there any witnesses?"

"No. Not at first."

"And later?"

"Later . . ."

Hermine stopped and took a few steps in the narrow space between the baby grand, the table-top bureau and the window. With her hand lying flat against her hips, she let herself go, her back humped and her chest hollow, as mannequins do when they're exhausted.

"I don't know why I'm telling you all this," she said. "Anyway, later he came in, Léon . . . Monsieur Weekend. Since I wasn't supposed to be there at that time, he was startled. Then Madame Lac—Madame Weekend—told him that I'd asked if I could leave the office because I wasn't well. From the way I looked, it might have been true."

"And what about the revolver?" *And what about the revolver?*

"She put it away in a drawer. The rotten thing. It doesn't work. You can imagine what I looked like, holding a thing that went *click* when I tried to fire . . ."

She went to look down into the street with an absentminded expression, chewing at her lipstick.

"But what about her?" Alice went on. "What did she look like?"

"She didn't look like anything. She twisted my wrist." She turned back her cuff slightly, then replaced it. "And she picked up the revolver. That's all. Oh, you don't know her."

"You said that Monsieur Weekend came in eventually? When you left, what did he do?"

"Nothing," said Hermine. "He's a man," she said with calm bitterness. "Have you ever seen a man do something at the exact moment when you expect him to?"

"Not often," said Alice. "But I've seen women do

things, as you say, which are very silly. You're not going to tell me . . ."

"Quiet, my dear, quiet. We're all childish in our own way."

The elder sister looked up in astonishment at the tall young woman in black who resembled her, apart from her fair hair and thin, anxious figure, who had never once thought of calling her "my dear," in a detached, superior tone of voice. She felt suddenly exhausted for no reason, stretched her legs out on the divan and longed for a cup of scalding hot coffee and the presence of Michel, the frivolous silence of Michel after luncheon, the rustling of the illustrated papers as Michel leafed through them. . . .

"Listen, Hermine . . ."

With a movement of her arm her younger sister rejected what she was about to say. "No. 'Listen, Hermine,' is the equivalent of 'You see, old chap,' which an experienced father hands out to his son. You've had no experience, Alice."

"I've had as much as you, though."

"Less than me. You've never undertaken the worst of women's tasks, making sure of a man. We four have slogged rather too much for four people, and we haven't enjoyed ourselves enough; and then, as for you, all you had to do was to let yourself fall into Michel's arms. Frankly, you didn't have to try very hard. I won't mention Bizoute. She's lost."

She stopped for a moment by the window, shivered perceptibly, and threw around her shoulders the rug with large checks—the *dipla*—which at night completed the bedclothes on the divan. As she did so, Hermine was thus resurrecting, before Alice's very eyes, the Alice of twenty-five who, draped in the same rug and standing by the same half-open window, would wait for three raucous blasts on the horn of a wretched, wheezy little motor car driven by Michel. . . .

"Love," Hermine went on, "doesn't need to struggle for existence when it's returned. There was no one between you and Michel for you to get rid of."

"But," said Alice, "you and Monsieur Weekend—isn't it love, then?"

Hermine shrugged her shoulders feverishly and clasped her hot cheeks between her hands.

"Yes . . . no . . . you must really think—"

"I'm sorry," Alice interrupted her. "There's no question of what I 'must think.' Gratuitous suppositions have never been part of our code. Any more than offensive inquisitions. If you'd ever stuck your nose, the prettiest nose in the family, and the least Annamite-looking, into my private life, I'd have sent you packing. And nobody's penetrated the silence, which wasn't very pleasant, that you kept about Monsieur Weekend, and you can go on keeping it now."

"It's high time," said Hermine, laughing sorrowfully. "Léon—Monsieur Weekend—he's—he's my opportunity—what can I tell you? He's my objective, an objective that presented itself; he's . . ."

"But he's married, Hermine!"

"That's not my fault, old thing. For two years I've

been thinking about it, I've been concentrating, I've been cautious, I've been studying myself, I've trained myself strictly—very strictly. I'm even jealous. If it's not love, damn it, it's as good as."

The harshness faded from her thirty-year-old face and she leaned toward Alice with the smile of a coquettish young girl. "You know, you mustn't think he's as bad as all that! In the first place, he's only forty-five, and—"

Alice interrupted her sharply. "But, you little fool, you don't seem to realize that you've just tried to shoot his wife, and it's all over!"

"Hush!" said Hermine, raising her finger knowingly. "Maybe not . . . maybe not . . ."

She was already glowing with energy. She had regained her color. She took off the rug, and between the window and the piano she paced up and down in the restricted space where they had grown up in a crowd together.

Then she sank down on the old divan. She looked limp and pale, her lips were dry, and her weakness showed even in her eyes. She lowered her eyelids and exhaled a long breath through her nose.

"I don't know if I'm on the wrong track," she murmured, "but it seems to me that it must be a big consolation to lose a man only because he's dead."

"That's the generally accepted opinion among women who haven't yet lost their husbands or their lovers," said Alice coldly. "May I know what you're going to do now? I'm going out to have some coffee."

"Me too."

As she stood up, the color of her cheeks changed and she leaned against the piano. "I'll be all right. Oh, first of all—just a moment, would you?" She leaned her elbows on the baby grand and pressed her hands against her temples. "Let's see, it was . . . a quarter to twelve when I left the two of them together. She has lunch with her daughter at home. But he nearly always eats in his staff canteen. If he's had lunch there today, lunch finishes at . . . one o'clock, ten past one. . . . What's the time, Alice?"

"Half past one."

"Either he's gone up to his office, or he's gone out for some fresh air. Has she told him everything, or hasn't she? I want to see him, let me . . ."

Harshly she carried out her telepathic mission, looking through walls and space, pressing her fingertips to her eyeballs.

"I think she'll have told him everything. She was so calm with me! But afterward she'll have relaxed and he'll have heard plenty! In that case he's in his office and he'll be waiting for me to phone him!" she said all in one breath.

With rapid, unsteady steps she ran toward her bedroom, where Alice heard the clicking of the telephone dial.

"Hullo . . . hullo . . . oh . . . yes, it's me. What? Yes, I thought so. What? . . . Oh, I don't mind, anywhere. . . . All right!"

She returned, transfigured. Her mouth orange, two

shades of powder on her face, her gray-green eyes full of excitement, boldly blond, beautiful with her large mouth and small nose: she filled Alice with astonishment.

"By Jove, the beautiful murderess!"

Hermine heard the word with an absentminded smile as she fastened her glove.

"Well? Did you get him?"

"Got him."

"Are things the way you thought?"

"Yes. She's told him."

"All the same, dear 'Mine, if you had killed her—where would you be? I wonder . . ."

"You have absolutely no imagination."

As she spread out her arms she seemed suddenly to be flying away, opening out in the shape of a cross, growing taller.

"Ah!" she cried. "He was waiting, beside the telephone! He said uh-hmm, uh-hmm, in his usual way, like a man who's embarrassed; he muttered heaven knows what. He said, 'Three o'clock,' he barely mentioned the thing, the weapon . . . click-click . . ."

Holding her arm stiff, crooking her index finger, she aimed at the wall. She let her hand drop again and looked affectionately at her sister.

"You see, Alice, everything's starting all over again! The marvelous unbearable life's starting all over again! Now this time, I assure you . . ."

She nestled against her sister, trembling like a leaf. Alice felt a protruding, emaciated hip against her side.

"Come here, you poor child. Come and be comforted."

Hermine ran down the stairs lightly. *What's going to become of her?* wondered Alice. *If the revolver had gone off. . . . What would Michel have said? Have I even had time to think of Michel since I've been here? Do I even want to think of Michel?*

She hurried along behind her sister, inhaling her scent and planning to talk to her with patience and authority. But she knew she would do nothing about it, and in comparison she found herself deprived and slightly envious.

The euphoria which had come to Hermine from drinking hot coffee faded quickly. As soon as the cuckoo-shaped pottery wall clock in the Café de la Banque et des Sports showed a quarter to three, she lost something of her sparkle.

"I'd like to see you eat something more than that spongy brioche," Alice told her.

"Good heavens! When I was a mannequin at Vertuchou's the professional mannequins always said that when they had a big show they preferred to do it more or less on an empty stomach rather than buck themselves up by eating a lot. But drinking didn't count. So down went tepid coffee and medium-sweet champagne. We were all so nervous and tired that it all came back, I can assure you, and quickly too."

She fell silent, looked in her mirror quickly, and stood up. "I'm going." She offered her gloved hand to Alice, her eyes elsewhere.

"Don't you want me to take you?"

"Oh, you know . . . it's hardly worth it. Well, all right, then; you can drop me off."

She gave the taxi driver the address of a bar in the rue Paul-Cézanne. During the ride she frowned and bit the insides of her cheeks with an air of concentration, as though she were going over a lesson. Through the door of the bar Alice had time to see a man rising quickly to his feet to greet Hermine.

The afternoon was long. About five o'clock she resigned herself to going back to her own apartment, where she opened the drawers of a desk and a chest. She found two or three telegrams, well hidden, which she destroyed with cool indifference. *They could have hurt Michel, if he'd found them. That Ambrogio business again! Wasn't I a good wife, then? Yes, I was, in fact. From the marital point of view I was as good as Michel. Neither of us imagined we were betraying the other. How nasty one is without knowing it. . . .*

She kept an eye on the open window, watching for the approach of evening, not wanting darkness to take her by surprise. She took care, too, not to give way to the sentimental hysteria which flows from a recent past, provoked by sheets of paper covered with writing, an old faint scent, the date of a postmark. As soon as she noticed that she was trembling slightly, she stopped going through bundles of documents and opening envelopes. She washed her hands and put on the hat with the short veil again.

Nobody's waiting for me anywhere; there's no hurry.

The word "waiting" produced a persistent image: Hermine and the man she had glimpsed, moving toward each other.

In the street she reduced the speed of her long strides as soon as the first lights appeared in the shop windows. The stationers, fruit shops and confectioners all revived the habit, the need, to "take something back for Michel," something nice, unnecessary, sweet. . . . *I can just as easily take something back for Colombe. And Hermine. . . . But Hermine and Colombe are where their personal priorities take them. One's working, and helping her friend who's poor, crushed by the burden of work and his wife. The other's conducting a full-scale fight with a man she's trying to turn into an ally. And I . . .*

She felt the onset of a desire to be faint-hearted, and clicked her tongue as Colombe did: "Tt,tt,tt," She bought fruit, smoked beef, rolls sprinkled with fennel seeds, and gâteaux. *If they're tired, it'll be fun to have dinner up there, with bare feet, as we used to. Yes, but when we used to do that there were four of us, even five, counting Father. Bread warmed up on the stove, mortadella and cheese, with cider to wash it down.*

A shudder of physical fear, out of the past, brought her the image of one Christmas Eve long ago: four Eudes daughters, in pale green pongee silk, engaged as orchestra in a café with a terrace from five o'clock in the afternoon until seven o'clock in the morning. *We daren't eat, I remember, for fear we might collapse on the floor asleep. I played the cello more like the double bass:* poum . . . poum . . . *tonic and dominant, tonic and dominant. Hermine, who was fifteen, was sick whenever she drank anything, and people applauded because they thought she was drunk. Colombe tried to beat a chap to death with a chair. And Bizoute—poor, wonderful Bizoute—at that time she used to pose for "art photographs" with a lyre, a missal, an elderly lion, and gigantic shadows of hands over her body . . .*

Yet she felt well disposed toward some evenings in the past which had brought together, in the warm depths of the toutounier, the four Eudes daughters in their precarious security, the most beautiful of them sometimes naked, the most delicate one covered with a long Venetian shawl. *It's a long time ago. It's gone now. Now Michel has already stopped sharing my fate, and Hermine has just tried to kill Madame Weekend.*

She proceeded thoughtfully to preparing a snack meal; she spread the worn little pink tablecloth on the desk and laid the places, putting the extra plates on the piano. *As usual . . . as we always did . . . oh, I've put one too many; there are only three of us now. Is it so difficult then to find homes for four girls like us and settle them somewhere? We're not bad, nor stupid, nor ugly; just a little stubborn. Seven o'clock. Where can Hermine be?* Nobody had ever asked, "Where can Colombe be?" Colombe, the inviolate, exhausted and indefatigable: was she not always where duty demanded, smoking and coughing? The familiar cough could be heard now outside, and Alice opened the door.

"I'm so glad, my dear toutounier girl, you're back

early! Not too worn out? Sit down there; put your big feet up. How's the Balabi? Will he come to see me? I've got lots to tell you! Nothing awful, luckily, as it happens. But do you know what Hermine has done?"

Briefly she described Hermine's attempted crime: "Fortunately the revolver jammed, or rather, I imagine, it wasn't loaded—*click-click.* At three o'clock Hermine was meeting Monsieur Weekend in the bar . . ."

As she spoke she dried her hands. She had just cut up the salad. "Aren't you pleased to hear the news?"

"Yes," said Colombe vaguely. "Of course."

Astonished, Alice looked more closely, beneath the band of hair, at the handsome, sad, masculine face which extreme fatigue imposed on her elder sister.

"Did you know, Colombe?"

"What? No, I knew nothing about it. After all . . . it's a normal kind of risk . . . one of the risks."

"What's the matter, Colombe? Aren't you well?"

The light-colored tired eyes met hers.

"I'm all right, but I don't know where I am. It's Carrine, you know . . . ."

Alice angrily threw her towel down on the piano.

"Oh, I see! It's Carrine now! What's happened this time? Have you quarreled? Has his wife died?"

Colombe shook her head patiently. "No question of that at the moment, unfortunately. No, Carrine has been offered the post of conductor for the musical season at Pau, the festivals at Biarritz and the premiere of a musical comedy at Biarritz, before Paris. And a salary . . ."

She whistled, passed her large hand through her hair and uncovered her white forehead.

"What's more, it appears that the restful atmosphere of the Basque country would be excellent for his wife. Restful!" she cried. "I'll give them restful!"

She coughed, and a flush of hostility passed over her features.

"How long would he be away?" asked Alice after a silence.

"I make it six months. Six months," sighed Colombe. "And to think I live on crumbs as it is . . . oh, I'm sorry, my dear."

She seized Alice's hand, pressing it against her dry mouth and then her cheek.

"When Hermine's not hurting you, I'm doing it. Ever since you've been here you've done nothing except bump into clumsy pieces of furniture. Besides . . ." She looked up at Alice innocently. "Besides, it's not the same for you. Nobody can take Michel away from you, nor take away what you had together."

"I know. Hermine's already had the foresight to point out to me the advantages of my situation."

The elder sister took hold of Alice's arms, made her sit down on the old divan and embraced her.

"My *jolie!* My little blue *guézézi!* My little *boudi!* Just see how badly everyone's treating you! My *picouciau* . . ."

They cried a little, won over by the old vocabulary of their childhood, by the need to laugh and to shed tears. But they did not give way for very long. Colombe returned to her role of the humble, worried woman in love.

"You realize, my *guézézi,* if Carrine goes, he has to decide tomorrow. It was very decent of Albert Wolff; he not only gave up the post, but he nominated Carrine and maneuvered the whole thing."

"Would you go too?"

The honest eyes looked away as she tried to lie.

"I don't see how I could. The first thing the Balabi did was to offer me a—a sort of very responsible secretarial job. Very worthwhile work, and technical. . . . You see, since we've been working together, I haven't been exactly useless to him," she added proudly. "But down there, what a hellish existence; his wife an invalid, blackmailing him with angina. . . . And then, if I go, I must have something to go with . . ."

Colombe's fingers, stained brown with nicotine, plucked intermittently at the brim of the worn felt hat she had placed beside her.

"You forget that I've got money, Colombe," said Alice after a silence.

She expected her sister to start, perhaps to cry out. But for too long Colombe had allotted only a very small place in her life to temptations. She heard the offer with a wise, incredulous smile which brought deep creases to her cheeks. She stroked Alice's shoulder and stood up.

"Leave things as they are. Until tomorrow. The Balabi has to give his answer tomorrow. Just now he's in his work corridor. He's walking up and down, like this. His two long strands of curly hair are flopping over his nose . . . he looks like a nearsighted ram, like this, and he's humming his final little incantation: 'I'm in a fix . . . I'm in a fix.' "

She was imitating the man she loved, the way he walked, the dispirited slope of his shoulders, his voice.

She can see through walls too, like Hermine, thought Alice. *How did I come to lose my second sight? A memory, a regret, a dead man: are they so little, then, besides their passion for the future? It will desert them.* . . . She concealed a little smile, but soon lost it and tried to punish herself for it: *In fact, we all feel ashamed if there's no longer a man in our lives. . . .*

"So you really love him still, Colombe?" she asked softly.

Colombe's honest, masculine eyes turned toward her. "I do, I really do, I assure you. He's defenseless; you know him," she added gently. She became gloomy and fished a mangled cigarette out of her pocket. "I know we're all naïve enough to believe that by loving a man we're diverting his attention from a woman who's worse than we are."

"Leave your *sisibecque* alone and come and eat. I've got two little bottles of your filthy sticky black beer under the tap. We're not going to wait for the other lunatic."

"Lovely! Stout!" cried Colombe. "Oh, but first of all, this very moment . . ."

She unfastened her long flat shoes and shook them off, removed her stockings and stood upright on two large naked feet, white and perfectly shaped, as lean as those of Christ on the cross. She looked at them in friendly fashion.

"They've covered a lot of ground again! This evening I walked back with the Balabi, and then he walked back here again with me. I'm going to put them under the tap as well. I've brought up *Paris-Soir.* Do you want it?"

She went into the bathroom, where Alice could hear her whistling. *She's whistling . . . she'll go.* Alice lay on the toutounier; her eyes left the open newspaper and followed the same paths as the previous day, stopping at the same vantage points, but the pleasure she had rediscovered then was already mingled with criticism. *I couldn't tolerate that black treelike shape where the smoke goes behind the pipe over the stove. And then this desk and all those messy papers. Michel and I couldn't bear a particular kind of untidiness, what I'll call the snobbery of untidiness. Tomorrow I'll attack that desk.* . . . Through the open window below the glass panel came a breath of May air. In the street the door of a taxicab banged with finality. *I'll bet . . . that sounds very like Hermine . . .*

"It's Hermine," confirmed Colombe, who brought with her from her quick shower the unsophisticated scent of lavender. She tied the cord of her bathrobe, opened the front door and called into the corridor, "I know everything! *He* was resisting you; you've murdered him!"

A hoarse peal of laughter answered her, and Colombe walked out barefoot to meet her sister, with whom she exchanged exclamations, cries of "You've been going a bit far!" whispered words and laughter. *They're crazy,* thought Alice, who hadn't moved; *or else I've lost the atmosphere of the place, and the notion that a murder that didn't come off can be funny.* The two sisters came in, arm in arm. *I've not seen them getting on so well together since I've been here, nor looking so pretty. . . .*

Colombe had looked beautiful as she emerged from the water and loosened her dark hair; now in her blue bathrobe she had a majestic radiance that Alice described as the "look of an archangel on a spree." She was supporting Hermine, who was leaning over and seemed to be dissolving and shrinking, admitting that she had reached the end of her tether. The black dress and beret, both with their golden brooches, were covered in dust. But an angry happiness isolated her face from her exhausted body, the face of a woman who was not renouncing her triumph. Alice sat up, facing her, and questioned her briefly. "Well, Hermine?"

"It's all right."

"What's all right? Is he going to get a divorce?"

Her younger sister's features clouded again. She let herself sink down into the large furrow which ran along the toutounier.

"Not so fast! Wait . . . the idiotic thing I've just done isn't turning out too badly, it seems. . . . I'm certain now, girls. The horizon's looking remarkably brighter!"

"Stop this muddled-up meteorology and explain it all clearly," complained Alice.

"In the first place, you've got to make allowances,"

moaned Hermine. "The only food I've had consists of two cocktails and two watercress sandwiches. The very man who's supposed to wish me well had the presumption to make me drink anisette with water and eat coffee éclairs. Whom can one trust?"

She laughed as she talked and took off her clothes without standing up, slipping out of her tight-fitting dress, removing a little pair of silk-knit knickers, a girdle with pink suspenders, long bronze-colored stockings. Just as she was about to slip off the shoulder straps of her very short petticoat she stopped, folded her arms over her breasts and looked at her two sisters pleadingly.

"If one of you will get my thick dressing-gown for me, I'll be your slave forever."

She was shivering with cold and nerves and a kind of shyness. While Colombe went to get the gown, Alice detected in Hermine's pale, pathetic eyes the abject desire, which she did not encourage, to take refuge in her arms.

A fine woolen dressing-gown with a pattern of embossed stitching fell over her quivering shoulders, and its pink glow rose to her cheeks, where the makeup had lost its delicate morning color beneath successive layers of powder.

"Stay where you are, you two," ordered Alice. "So many things have happened to you since this morning. . . ."

She organized the little meal on her own, ordering wine, bread and ice by telephone from the brasserie next door. She enjoyed her work and felt relieved at escaping a new edition of the "Weekend affair" and the timid remarks of Colombe. Her two sisters made no move to help her, moreover. As she came and went, she heard snatches of their detailed stories; they were "women to whom so much had happened."

"From one point of view," Colombe was saying, "my Balabi would feel freer at Pau, and so would I, since work would force us to be together. This would make our friendship legitimate in a way, you understand . . ."

Hermine agreed, nodding her head firmly, saying, "Mm . . . mm . . ." at regular intervals. "And Colombe doesn't even notice that Hermine's thinking of something else," laughed Alice. She uncorked the wine, broke up the ice and poured the unmanageable stout and its fawn-colored froth into a carafe.

"I don't maintain," cried Hermine, "that what I did was a stroke of genius, but . . ."

Alice polished the glasses and shrugged her shoulders. *Oh yes she does. She's on the point of saying so! If it works out well, she'll even go as far as to say that she hadn't loaded the revolver. . . .* With an effort she abandoned her carping—that of someone newly deprived—clapped her hands and uttered the sacred call:

> To table! To table!
> Let's eat what's in the pot
> Which will be quite detestable
> If it's not eaten hot!

The urgent need to eat made them silent at first. Brief, understanding smiles passed from one to another; there were words of thanks to Alice, while cries greeted the sparkling wine and the coolness of the butter swimming among the icebergs in iced water. The smoke from the cigarettes—no sooner did Colombe put one out than Hermine or Alice lit another—spoiled the taste and smell of the food. But from the time of their adolescence the three sisters hadn't noticed it. When they had eaten enough they continued to drink slowly, crumbling their gâteaux into small pieces, while Colombe, like Hermine, began to look different. The archangel on the spree became a worried archangel, and Hermine neurotically scratched the bright red varnish on her thumbnail.

"Haven't you any coffee?" she asked Alice.

"You didn't order any."

Hermine extended her slender arm from the thick pink sleeve in apology.

"But my dear toutounier girl, it's quite simple! Colombe, I bet you'd like some coffee? Yes? Colombe, whistle!"

Colombe sat on the sill of the open window and emitted a long whistle, ending with three detached notes. From the street came an identical signal.

'The Café de la Banque et des Sports is sending us up three filters," said Hermine. "It's simple. As you see, we've organized some comfort here. I'm terribly humiliated, because I've never been able to whistle. At Vertuchou's the mannequins used to say that women who couldn't whistle were frigid!"

Inexplicably she was overcome with hysterical laughter and then fell silent until the thick brown coffeepot arrived. Lazily Colombe rinsed the three glasses in the ice bucket like some casual old waiter, and filled them with warm coffee. Hermine became anxious again and replied, "No, no sugar . . . no thank you," and "Yes, two lumps . . ." alternately. Cigarette ash and stubs piled up in the black glass bowl.

"You drink too much coffee, Hermine."

"Leave her alone," said Colombe. "*Sisibeques* and coffee are food for the Eudes girls. So much has happened to them!"

"Not to me," said Alice. "At least, not today."

Her two sisters looked at her with embarrassment. *No doubt they'd forgotten that Michel's dead,* she thought. *It's not for me to reproach them.*

"Children, we've reached a turning point in our history. Hermine, I'd so much like to know what you're going to—what you think you're going to do . . ."

Hermine looked down, pursing her lips. "Don't worry about it more than you need," she said, with constraint. "We didn't ask you any questions when you left the team."

"It's not the same thing, 'Mine. I was marrying Michel, and that was all."

"Well, assume that I'll be marrying Léon . . . and that's all."

"Good heavens, child, that doesn't sound very friendly . . ."

The sound of the telephone bell interrupted; it hit Hermine so violently that she didn't rush toward it at once but remained motionless, her dressing-gown open over her chest, her eyes fixed on the bedroom door. Then she jumped up, caught her flowing garment on the corner of the table and, rather than lose time, slipped out of it angrily and ran almost naked toward the telephone. Alice looked at Colombe and shook her head.

"A cave-woman," she said. "Who would have believed it?"

They were silent, smoking as they drank the remaining coffee. From Hermine's bedroom came interrupted sentences, clipped words uttered very loudly, murmured phrases. One silence was so long that Alice became anxious. But the monologue began again in a lower key, calm now and wary.

"What can they be saying to each other?" asked Alice.

Colombe was thinking of other things and did not hear. Her head was leaning on her hand, her black hair half-concealing her cheek, and she was looking at the dark window with gentle feminine eyes, submissive and clear. *She's talking to* him, *she too* . . . For the first time since her arrival Alice had to fight hard against the tightening in the throat, the salty saliva that comes before sobs. From Hermine's room came a cry as triumphant as the last cry of a woman in labor, and a moment later Hermine reappeared. Unsteadily she picked up her fleecy dressing-gown and clutched it to her. As she climbed over the back of the sofa her icy naked foot touched Alice's hand.

"Shouting like that," grumbled Colombe, who was attentive now, "—it's enough to make the milk turn sour."

"What's happened, Hermine?"

Hermine looked at her sisters, her pale face streaked with ocher and rouge, her eyes filled with big round glistening tears.

"He said—he said . . . ," she stammered, "he said that—that he would get a divorce, that we'd be married . . . that we'd go a long way away . . . together. . . ."

The big luminous tears brimmed over. Against Alice's shoulder rested a naked shoulder, a shower of fair hair and the feverish scent extracted from a woman by deep emotion, and the heaviness of a body which, once disarmed, recovers all its weight again.

Alice straightened herself in order to support her flagging sister more easily; she nursed her vaguely and let her sob.

"Are you sure at least . . ." she ventured to say after a moment.

"Sure?"

A red nose parted the golden hair; Hermine, ugly, happy, all shiny with tears, was indignant. "Sure! How can you . . . a man who's going to turn his whole life upside down, who's got his wife to ask for a divorce, a man like that . . ."

It's a classic situation, thought Alice. *She's already proud of the harm she's done and the unhappiness she's causing.*

"And just think, Colombe," cried Hermine, in a

changed voice, "he only told me at the end of the telephone call that she'd asked for a divorce! Oh," she muttered, her laughter full of angry admiration, "I don't know what I'll do to him! Colombe, can you believe it?"

She appeals only to Colombe, thought Alice. *I'm out of it completely.*

"He's full of spite," admitted Colombe. "And what does he mean by going a long way away?"

"I don't know," said Hermine, who was busy powdering her ruined face, smoothing her eyebrows and eyelashes with a wet finger. She remained thoughtful, her mirror and her powder compact in her hands. "Madeira, perhaps . . ."

Her loose hair lay over her naked shoulder. She was gazing into the void at a future which chance had just saved, and at Madeira, with its golden name, its golden wine. . . .

"Madeira?" repeated Colombe. "Why Madeira? What an odd idea."

Hermine looked at her sister with childish malice. "I'd say it's about as good as Pau!"

She burst out laughing, and Colombe followed her example an octave lower.

They're acting together, thought Alice. *At the moment they belong to the same cast. For how long?* The laughter stopped. Hermine turned to Alice with over-obvious kindness. "We're really upsetting you today . . ."

I embarrass them . . . I'm the odd one out. They won't

dare show off in front of each other anymore when I'm here. . . .

When three knocks were heard at the door Hermine jumped, but Colombe lowered her eyes and stood up without surprise.

"It's Carrine. He told me that if there were any developments he'd come . . . provided that . . ."

She tied the cord of her bathrobe, fixed her hair behind her right ear and opened the door. Carrine, with his goatlike profile, tall, thin and lost in an off-white raincoat, went first to Alice.

"Alice, my dear friend . . ." He embraced her, putting his arms around her, then stepped back to look at her. "I'm very pleased you're so beautiful. Beauty is the best sign . . ."

"Well, the Balabi's clumsy, but he knows very well what to say." Alice smiled at the goatlike face, the hair in corkscrew curls, light-colored and mingled with white, the very fine brown eyes that were slightly protuberant and perpetually full of entreaty. Hermine said "Hullo, Balabi" to him as if he were a little boy. Colombe said nothing; but she helped him take off his raincoat, which she folded with care, then sat down and pulled the hem of her bathrobe down as far as her faultless big toes.

"Hermine, fasten up your dressing gown," whispered Alice in her sister's ear.

Hermine obeyed, but not without a glance of utter derision: *For him? Is it worth it?*

From Carrine's hesitancy, Alice realized that he was

trying to make an appropriate remark about Michel's death, and she wanted to relieve him of this concern.

"Lots of new developments, Balabi, I gather? Colombe's told me . . . Pau, the conducting job, Biarritz and everything?"

"Yes . . . in fact, I've come—I'm disturbing you . . ."

"No, old *zog.* It's a very good offer, isn't it?"

"Yes. In fact . . . oh, it's not that I'm afraid it's beyond my professional capacity . . ."

He was looking at Colombe, and his complete lack of vanity touched Alice, while at the same time it exasperated her a little. *He hasn't got enough chin: that's what it is. He needs more chin. Just a little more squareness in the lower part of his face—and the shoulders—and Carrine would be a handsome man, perhaps a great man.*

As she examined this old friend, she rediscovered her terrible gift for criticism, an independent clairvoyance which had been inactive since Michel's death and the legal squabbles that had followed it. Carrine's presence, Colombe's modest face and girlish gentleness brought Alice back to a normal preoccupation with men. She compared Carrine's hock-bottle shoulders, over which his jacket hung loosely, with Michel's pectoral muscles and Lascoumettes's impressive back. Fleetingly she saw again Michel's former associate, Ambrogio, who would fall silent in admiration at the contrast between a very black fringe and a pair of horizontal gray-green eyes. A life-giving tide of egoism and coquetry returned, bearing Alice up. *What, because of Carrine? Well, yes! Because of Carrine and these two besotted girls. . . .*

Hermine, seated in a corner of the toutounier, her legs folded beneath her, studied the Balabi disdainfully. *She's thinking that her man's better. That remains to be seen. Mine too was better. But Colombe thinks the Balabi's a pearl from Golconda. What's Carrine saying, now?*

"The Casino manager came back while we were—while I was just starting my meal; my wife doesn't eat —I mean she's on a very strict diet, and it hasn't led to much improvement . . ."

The archangel in the bathrobe bestowed on him a dazzling, hard look, and then recovered her gentleness, lowering her eyes.

"He asked me to do him a personal favor by giving my answer immediately, since we'd agreed—hadn't we, Colombe?—about the terms, so I had to come, and I apologize, to ask Colombe . . ."

He spoke in a voice so well modulated that it discouraged any interruption, and Alice listened to him appreciatively. Colombe had turned her musician's ear toward him; even Hermine lost her thin-lipped smile, and her head approved the sound if not the words.

What's going to be decided this evening, thought Alice, *is not only the fate of these two women who're in love, but also my own solitude. For they'll both leave. They're leaving already. We never resist a man. Death is the only place where we don't follow him. . . .*

"So I'd like to know how you feel about it, Alice?"

She smiled at the questioner and didn't make him repeat what she had barely heard.

"But I think it's all fine, old *zog.* Fine for you and fine for Colombe."

"Do you? Really?"

"Really. Colombe, you know what I told you."

She realized that her elder sister had not yet said a word. *This silence . . . how faithful she is, and ready for everything, for this not handsome man, this second-class martyr, this timid Panlike creature—well, this decent chap, after all. . . .*

Carrine was standing. He shook Colombe's hand without any further effusions. She straightened his tie, pulled down the back of his badly cut jacket and said merely, "If you haven't time tomorrow, I'll go to Enoch's for you."

"Yes," said Carrine, "but it's not urgent. Oh, on the contrary, yes, it is urgent. . . ."

"Very well," said Colombe. "Not before six o'clock. I've got three lessons."

"Oh, your lessons, now . . ."

They exchanged a happy look, like two innocent practical jokers. Hermine said, "Good night, Balabi!" in her usual way to Carrine, and the three Eudes sisters were alone again.

"Ooooh!" yelled Hermine.

"What?" asked Colombe, turning her whole body toward her.

"Nothing. I'm hot."

She threw off her dressing-gown and stretched her

thin body, the paleness of a brunette with blond hair. Colombe poured herself a glass of water, drank it in one go, and furiously scratched her head with both hands.

Their impatience, thought Alice. *They're like people itching to go. They're like poor girls of thirty-five and twenty-nine who're destined to escape nothing, neither happiness nor unhappiness. They think their whole life's beginning today.*

"Oh!" cried Hermine. "Oh for some hot water! A bath!"

"You have it," conceded Colombe. "You've earned it."

She began to move about again in her deliberate, energetic way. She collected glasses and plates on a tray and carried them into the kitchen. Alice did the same, swept away the crumbs with the back of her hand, put some blue paper over the adjustable lamp on the piano, and spread the English sofa with sheets. They both worked skillfully without bumping into each other, exchanging words which came from far back in their adolescence.

"Stick your dress in the *padirac;* you can brush it tomorrow morning."

"Here, catch the *dipla;* fold it in two on the toutounier."

Hermine came back, frighteningly pale, staggering with fatigue. But she had taken the trouble to cover her face with rich cream and had rolled up her hair in curls beneath a coarse net. She murmured feebly, "Good night, ladies and gentlemen," pulled a face, blew a kiss and disappeared. Just as she joined her sister, who was already in bed, Alice hesitated:

"Will I get in your way? You'll need to move about, to think . . ."

As she lay there Colombe spread out her arms and smiled serenely: "Why, dear girl? Since everything's been settled, thank goodness, I'm not thinking about anything at this time of night."

"Does that mean that you're not thinking of yourself anymore? Sensible Colombe, you're jumping into the water in the wake of a man . . ."

Anxiety and qualms of conscience returned to the archangel's fine wide-set eyes.

"Oh, you know . . . I think, on the contrary, that I'm committing my first act of selfish delinquency. Just think, it's hardly ever happened to me, being able to choose what I like best. To go away, like this, to work a little more closely with Carrine; it's really what I'd have chosen, if I'd been given the choice. Thank you very much for . . . I hope I'll be able to give back what you'll be lending me."

"How intelligent!" said Alice sharply. "And especially, how kind. Paragraph seven of the toutounier code . . ."

"What's yours is mine, what's mine is yours," Colombe went on. "The wording has to be revised, in fact. Can you see Bizoute making me a present of her Bouttemy?"

"And me taking the Balabi for myself? Yes, the wording has to be revised. . . . Colombe, you're embarking on something difficult . . ."

She stretched out her hand, for the pleasure of touching Colombe's hair, which became soft when it was smooth and damp, like a horse's flank, Alice used to say.

"It's more difficult than being someone's mistress. In fact, why aren't you the Balabi's mistress?"

"I don't know," said Colombe. "I was afraid it would make complications."

"Don't you want to be?"

With a movement of her head Colombe let her hair slip down over her face. "Sometimes I think I do, sometimes I think I don't . . ."

"Has he asked you, since the old days?"

"Yes," said Colombe, embarrassed. "Only, since the old days, as you say, perhaps he thinks about it less . . . and then, we haven't got anywhere for that kind of encounter, and no little bachelor's flat."

"And what about this?" said Alice, striking the old sofa with the flat of her hand.

Colombe sat up indignantly.

"On the toutounier!" she cried. "Do that on the toutounier! I'd rather wear a chastity belt all my life! Our toutounier, it's so pure . . ." she said with sudden grace.

She didn't finish, blushed, and began to laugh in order to excuse her modesty.

"Alice, if we stay that way, the Balabi and I, without . . . does that make a strong enough bond between us?"

She was laughing, but her eyes were full of perplexity and a painful ignorance.

"Very strong," Alice assured her sagely. "A bond of

. . . superior quality. You can believe me."

"Oh! I believe you," said Colombe hastily. "But if, on the contrary, when we're down there, Carrine—"

"—becomes a satyr in disguise? That will be fine too."

"Oh . . ."

Colombe pondered, twisting around her nose the longest strand of hair that hung down from her forehead. "But how do you explain why two such different possibilities can both produce good results?"

"Damn it," said Alice. "Problems of that sort drive you mad. Move over a little, and let's go to sleep. What a day!"

Colombe gave one last cough, stubbed out her final cigarette and moved to the back of the toutounier. Alice put the lamp out, lay down, then bent her knees slightly. Two long legs clad in men's pajamas clung to her own, and almost immediately she heard her sister's long-drawn breathing as she fell asleep.

From the street, through the half-open window, came loud, disconnected sounds and vague gleams of light. A pale square of shadow on the ceiling indicated the position of the glass panel. Cold, soft hair fell from Colombe's forehead onto the back of Alice's neck, and she accepted its contact with a gratitude that was near to tears. *And what will it be like when she's gone? When they've both gone?"*

The feeling of someone close to her brought back no memory of marriage. As Michel's wife she had allowed only twin beds, apart from the time of actual lovemaking. Sometimes, if she had dozed off unexpectedly at Michel's side, she had forgotten where she was sleeping and had spoken to one of the band: "Move over, Colombe. Bizoute, what time is it?" But on the native toutounier, when a long arm had fallen over her sleep, Alice had never sighed, "Leave me now, Michel . . ."

A vague plan, engendered by the fear of losing everything that had been the communal possession of four girls without a mother, occupied her mind and kept her awake. *To come back here . . . stay here. Clean up and restore the favorite old hideout. For myself? No, for them too. Maybe they'll come back. Maybe I won't be waiting for them very long. Perhaps I could be waiting for someone else?* She answered this last conjecture with a curt denial, severe toward everything implied by the presence of an unknown man. Lying on her arm, which was folded back, she cradled in her hand a youthful naked breast untouched by its thirty-odd years, a breast that was slightly flat and very young. Distrustfully she banished from her thoughts the suspect prudery of widows. A sudden shower of rain with its pond-like smell calmed her, and she slept in the belief that she could not sleep.

Before dawn she was awakened by the intrusion of a slim body whose owner whimpered softly and slipped across the big bumpy sofa with the skill of an insinuating animal.

"Oh, all right," grumbled Colombe. "It's you. Go into the other corner, then. Don't wake Alice too much. And don't scratch us with your feet."

Alice pretended to be unaware of her youngest sister's presence and the well-clad body which sought, perhaps for the last time, the protection of the mingled limbs, the untamed chaste habit of sleeping together. She turned over, as though in a dream, placed her hand on a little round head, recognizing the scent of the blond hair. Yet the only name that rose to her lips was that of the fourth daughter, lost far away on the other side of the world. Her arm groped about and encountered a raised knee, a warm shoulder, shipwrecked here and there in darkness and sleep. . . .

"Is that you, Bizoute? Bizoute, are you there?"

"Yes," sighed Hermine's voice.

Alice accepted the affectionate lie and went to sleep again.